THE
WOUNDLESS
WAR

THE
WOUNDLESS
WAR
EARTH'S SECRET ALLIANCE

FRANK JONES: EPISODE 1

TONY B. RICHARD
AND LYDIA PAYGE

First Edition, October 2025

Cover designed by Sandra Drawz
Interior designed & edited by Carolin Petersen
Titles typeset in Kallisto

ISBN 978-1-0688457-6-5 (paperback)
ISBN 978-1-0688457-7-2 (ebook)

visit *www.tonybrichard.com*

Dedicated to my wife, Lydia, who has stood by my side through thick and thin. This book would not be possible without her.

Also dedicated to all people who persevere in the face of bullying, and those who are different in any way. Know that you are loved.

TABLE OF CONTENTS

CHAPTER ONE

TOP SECRET

ROSWELL ARMY AIRFIELD
July 8, 1947

"**P**lease help me fix this. The people around here are hard workers; they deserve better," General Frank Jones said quietly as he looked at multiple reports of the first nuclear tests and the effects of the radiation. Horrific photos marked TOP SECRET. Several depicted cattle suffering from birth defects. The rest of the papers contained purchase invoices for those cattle.

He glanced at a memo he had received that morning about an incident at Ashcroft Ranch. A team had been sent out to investigate. He felt tingles, and the hairs on the back of his neck raised as he heard a knock at the door.

"Enter," he called.

Lieutenant Hansley opened the door. He stood at attention and saluted.

After decades, Jones was tired of the constant salutes, but it was protocol. So, halfheartedly and dismissively, he raised his hand to his forehead, then dropped it. "What happened at the ranch?"

"How did you know, sir?"

Jones raised a single eyebrow but didn't answer.

"I have a message from Lieutenant Monroe. He requests your presence at the ranch with the crashed object. He also requested that you put the base on alert," Hansley said.

"Did he say what they found?"

"No, sir; he did not want to say it over the radio."

"Probably a good thing, but we don't know what we are dealing with, and I don't want to cause a panic." Jones thought for a moment. "Let's run an Alpha alert drill and let him know we will be right there. Also inform Trinity; this might be a distraction to steal our nuclear technology."

CHAPTER TWO

THE RANCH

ASHCROFT RANCH, ROSWELL

Jones invited Colonel George Liam with him to the crash site. "What do you think we will find?" he asked, getting straight to business.

"If they called you out, I would expect a Soviet spy plane," Liam replied.

As they arrived at the ranch, Jones saw hundreds of foil fragments. The driver parked the limousine beside the military trucks, and Jones saw what looked like a shredded fifty-foot foil umbrella. He stepped out of the car.

Sweat dripped down Lt. Monroe's pasty white face as he approached and saluted. "Sir, you're going to want to see this."

Holding back his annoyance, Jones returned the salute. "Yes, what is it, Lieutenant?"

"Aliens, sir."

"Aliens?" Jones raised an eyebrow. "Are they alive?"

"No, sir."

"Shame." He motioned Monroe to lead the way. The lieutenant's feet were fast and nervous, but Jones and Liam easily kept up. The way to the crash site had already been cleared of foil, so no one was around to overhear their conversation.

As he walked, Monroe turned his upper body to address the general. His eyebrows were scrunched. "Shame, sir?"

"Yes. It's going to be hard to find out why they're here if we can't talk to them."

Monroe's face reddened. "Does it matter, sir? They are foreigners on US soil," he protested.

"What would be your course of action?"

Monroe huffed. "For Pete's sake, General! Prepare for an invasion, of course! Mount a counteroffensive. If any more of these freaks show up, we should be blasting them out of the sky."

"Settle down, Lieutenant!" Liam warned.

Jones, however, was eager for Monroe to continue. "Attack? Who? Where?" he asked.

Monroe's face was redder than ever, but he didn't say anything, so Jones turned to Liam. "Do you agree with this assessment?"

Before Liam had a chance to answer, they reached the umbrella-like structure and ducked inside. The sight seemed to steal Liam's words as his mouth dropped open. Jones drew closer to the upside-down cone-like container. He hummed. It was covered in depictions of the allied flags. The door on the other side had a large American Flag printed on it.

"It has an American Flag front and center on the door, and you want to mount a counteroffensive?" Jones asked pointedly. He shook his head in disgust, then opened the door, exposing three small gray bodies with big heads and slanted, swollen eyes. "Who has seen this?"

"Just Privates Dow and Rabinowitz, and myself," Lt. Monroe replied. "The others might've caught a glimpse from a distance."

"Where are the privates now?"

Monroe pointed toward the hills. "They were last seen heading out that way to collect foil."

"Did you find any weapons?" Jones asked.

"No sir. Not yet. But I'm sure we will."

"Tell me, Lieutenant, does the aliens' clothing look more like a military uniform, a farmer's, or a monk's?"

Monroe spluttered. "A-a monk, sir…?"

"Yes, a monk. You know, those religious people who lead a simple life and dedicate their lives to serving God?"

Monroe stared back blankly.

Liam scrutinized the aliens with calculated interest. "He may have a point. Sir."

"How so?"

Liam's face was also blank.

"You're all ready to go to war, but you can't provide me with a reason to do so?" Jones looked at their blank faces again then shook his head. "I want to keep this under wraps. I don't see anything to suggest the invasion you say we should prepare for," he said. "I'm certain they've been following the results of the war and the peace treaty. This seems more like refugees in a rowboat scenario, and I don't want to cause a panic."

He alternated looking the two officers in the eye. "I am classifying this Top Secret. We will investigate, and I will report the preliminary findings directly to the president tomorrow. You are not to discuss this with anyone other than myself. Is that understood?"

The two officers straightened. "Yes, sir."

"Good. Now I want you to put these into body bags, and take them to…" Jones scanned the area. He pointed. "That barn. Ask the farmer to remove his animals and call the local veterinarian to do a house call."

"Sorry, sir. You don't want the base doctor, sir?" Monroe asked, his face red again.

"A human doctor is only familiar with humans. I want someone who has experience with other biologics as well."

Monroe bit his lip. "Yes, sir."

"I've also acquired a safe house, a local abandoned warehouse, for just such emergencies. Liam, take everything to this address. Only use senior personnel *whom you trust*." Jones handed the colonel a piece of paper and looked him in the eye, stressing his last words. "And escalate to Bravo alerts at the base and at Trinity. Understood?"

Liam gave a slight nod. "Yes, sir!"

"Dismissed."

CHAPTER THREE

AUTOPSY

ASHCROFT RANCH, ROSWELL

L t. Monroe and Col. Liam were already observing the veterinarian's procedure when Gen. Jones entered. "What can you tell me, doctor?"

The vet, Dr. Fisher, shook his head, looking lost. "I suppose you're the one I have to thank for this?"

"Yes, well…. What did you find?"

"They're definitely not like anything I've seen before."

Jones was expecting as much. He could see that Dr. Fisher was disappointed in his own assessment, but there was also a glint of interest in his eyes that brought Jones comfort. "Anything else?"

"Well, if I didn't know better, I would say that they were never born."

"What makes you say that?"

The doctor moved back toward the makeshift work-table and pointed to the bodies. "The skin is soft and pliable like a newborn baby, and the lungs and bones are not fully developed, like a stillborn calf."

"Could that be part of their species?"

"I don't see how."

Jones walked around the bodies. "Any idea what killed them? The physical trauma of the crash? Possibly a lack of oxygen?"

"As I said before, I'm not sure that they were alive in the first place. But if they were, my best guess would be suffocation."

"Thank you, Doctor," Jones replied. "You can go now, but remember not to tell *anyone* about this." He leveled the man with a serious look, recognizing the ambition in his eyes. Fisher was reluctant to go. Even if he didn't know much, the aliens clearly intrigued him far more than they spooked him.

The doctor shook his head with a haggard laugh. "Who would believe me?"

After he left, Jones turned to the officers. "Assessment?" Both of them were silent, so Jones asked, "Do you believe that they are a threat?"

Liam spoke first. "These ones, no sir. But where did they come from, and are there more of them, sir?"

"And are the other ones a threat?" Monroe added.

"Recommendations?" Jones asked.

"Gee willickers. As I said before, prepare for an invasion," Monroe answered. "Mount a counteroffensive.

The flags may be trying to lull us into a false sense of security, sir."

Jones was starting to get annoyed with Monroe's paranoia. He stared hard at his inferior officer. "Based on what? How are we going to prepare? Where are we going to attack?"

Monroe paused, thrown by the question, and Jones thought that was the end of it, but then Monroe said, "In space, sir."

Jones couldn't help but smile. "In space? And how are we going to get there? We don't have any vehicle capable of going to space. And what if they are friendly, as the pictures and flags suggest? Do you want to start a war with a technologically advanced species? How do you plan on winning a war when we can't even leave our planet?"

Monroe opened his mouth, but he said nothing. After a moment, he closed his mouth again. His Adam's apple bobbed as he swallowed hard.

Jones nodded. *Just as I thought.* "Lieutenant, you are dismissed." After he left, Jones turned to Col. Liam. "Take these bodies to the warehouse. I'll return to the base and book a personal appointment with the president."

Liam blinked. "A personal appointment, sir?"

"Yes, I want to brief the president in private. He can decide what to do from there."

"What about the Secretary of War and the Joint Chiefs?"

"As of right now, this is not an act of war, and therefore not their jurisdiction. And if we do bring it to them, we know what their response will be. Like Monroe, they will want to shoot first and ask questions later. Do you have a problem with an elected president deciding if we want to start an interplanetary war?"

Liam looked straight ahead, trying not to move, but Jones could see very subtle twitches. *He's going to be trouble. He masks it well, but I've seen that twitch before—on officers wrestling with their conscience, caught between duty and what they believe deep down.* "I'll tell you what. You can write your recommendation and I'll see to it that the president gets it."

Liam tilted his head. "Sir?" Then he regained his composure and stood at attention. "Thank you, sir!"

"Dismissed."

CHAPTER FOUR

OLD FRIENDS

WASHINGTON, D.C.

Jones entered the Oval Office. The smell of pine oil filled his nostrils, which was nicer than the cigar smoke of the previous occupant.

"Frank." President Whitmore rose from behind the desk.

"Mr. President." Jones saluted. He had known Whitmore since the start of their military careers. It was hard being formal and calling each other by titles rather than first names, but their jobs required professionalism.

"I thought this was a personal visit," said Whitmore.

"I'm sorry to deceive you, sir. It's urgent."

The president's brow furrowed. "That bad?"

"Worse."

Whitmore begrudgingly returned the salute. "Then let's sit." He pointed to the two white leather sofas and took a seat.

Jones settled on the velvety white sofa across from him. He drew a breath. "Yesterday, a team from my base was called to investigate the crash of an unidentified flying object. Inside were three non-human bodies with unusually big heads and eyes."

Whitmore gaped. "What? Are you talking *aliens*? And you brought this to me? Without the Joint Chiefs?"

Jones handed him a folder marked *Top Secret* and a sealed envelope. "I promised Colonel Liam that I would deliver his concerns to you."

Whitmore grunted as he opened the envelope. His eyes ran over the paper as a few words escaped his lips. "General Jones...reckless...horrible mistake... Secretary of War and the Joint Chiefs...prepare for invasion, counteroffensive...impeachment.... You obviously disagree with his assessment."

Jones chuckled. "Yes, sir. Are you or the warmongers going to confirm the existence of aliens?"

"Of course not. After that radio drama ten years ago, there would be panic in the streets."

"So, no impeachment, no investigation."

The president nodded. "Ah...I see.... OK, I get your point. Give me the facts."

Jones had expected this and had already prepared his answers. "A small ship crash landed in Roswell, New Mexico, about a hundred miles from the Trinity nuclear test site, and the debris indicates it came from that direction."

Jones paused to let the information sink in. Then, he continued. "They're no threat, Mr. President; they were unarmed. The thing that crashed was a lifeboat, not a warship."

"How can you be certain?"

"If it were a military probe, they'd have been in uniform, carrying weapons, maybe even injured, to test our response. Instead, the bodies were small, like children, and were dressed like monks. The entire hull was covered in Allied flags and images of the Allied leaders. They've been watching us and are trying to communicate. That's not an invasion. That's a plea."

The president nodded slowly. "I see, but what do they want?"

"With everything I've learned so far, it's clear that they're interested in our weapons, but they don't want to just take them and leave. They need us too. They want our help."

Whitmore balked at Jones. "Help? They can travel between planets, and they want our help? What could they possibly want from us?"

"Their lifeboat indicates they are escaping a war, a war that they are losing. I'm sure they've created a refugee situation to see who is sympathetic to them, and who is not." Jones paused. "But they're not trying to settle here. By trying to land at the Trinity nuclear test site, unarmed, I believe they are asking for our help fighting that war."

"You always astound me with your deductions. What do we do from here?"

"The war is clearly one-sided. If they were the aggressors, they'd have just stolen what they needed from us and left already. If they're coming here, that means they can't fight for themselves, or their enemy is just as advanced as them and they're losing ground too fast. The fact that they're here means that whoever is attacking them can get here too. If our visitors lose their war, I'm certain that we'll be next. We should first make contact. Ally with the aliens that are here, merge their technology with ours, and—"

"*Ally* with them?" Whitmore shot forward on the sofa, his eyes wide and incredulous.

"Yes, Mr. President. If I'm right, their technology is the only way to defend Earth."

Whitmore stood up. "Are you serious? First, you talk about the aliens not being invaders, and now you're convinced that there *are* invaders on the way? And the only way we can stop them is by helping these guys who opened the floodgates to begin with?"

"Sir," Jones said, voice so calm and collected that it eased some of the president's nerves. "We must always be prepared, but we must not panic. The future will always be full of scary things, but it's how we react to it that makes all the difference."

"I know that, but this?"

"Nothing is certain. I very well may be wrong, but

what chance would we have against their advanced technology anyway? That would be like us fighting with swords against a B-29 Superfortress." Jones leaned forward, gesturing for the president to sit down again.

With a softer voice, Jones said, "If they wanted to attack us, they would have. We have no way to defend against the speed of an interplanetary spacecraft. We need to focus on what we know, and what *I* know is that we haven't found the slightest sign of anything military. With everything else: the flags, the images, the clear refugee scenario…."

"Hmm…I see your point," Whitmore said, dabbing at his sweating brow with a handkerchief. "But…ally with an alien race we know nothing about, and fight a war we know nothing about?"

"Not entirely true, sir," Jones said. "We know *these* aliens didn't attack or steal from us, sir. They are reaching out to us with images that we understand."

"True." The president nodded, then paused, then suddenly shook his head. "But you must be crazy. Allying with aliens? No, *definitely* not!"

Jones hummed. *Why is he resisting? What could worry him so much? Is he worried about what the public will think of him? I can't deny that it's a reasonable concern. Heck, half the people already can't stand the other half. What would they think of aliens?* He stared, hard, at the president. *How can I counter this fear?*

Jones spoke softly, "Would you rather deal with their technologically advanced, aggressive enemy?"

"Well…." The president looked down. His eyes moved rapidly. "Are you willing to lead this battle? In space? With an enemy that you know nothing about?"

Jones sat up tall. *Now we're getting somewhere.* "I would be honored, sir! I don't see that we have much of a choice. Defending others and defending the United States—*that's* what I signed up for when I joined the army. And I have to defend Earth to do that."

"You're certain? You're putting a lot of faith in this guess of yours, Frank."

Frustration clawed at Jones. He'd thought he explained it clearly. "Not a guess, sir," he said firmly. "I made my decision with facts and that gut instinct of mine that you've always trusted."

"A hunch!" The president shook his head. "You are willing to put the future of this country, this *planet*, on a *hunch*?"

"There were lots of facts. My hunch just backs them up. Do you think that I'm wrong, sir?"

Whitmore paused, then rose and walked over to his desk. He faced away from Jones for a moment, fingers dancing across the wood. He picked up the brass name plate then set it back down. Finally, he turned back to Jones.

"Unfortunately, I do not. As usual, your reasoning is sound, and like you said, I've always trusted your gut."

Jones nodded sharply. "Thank you, sir."

"OK, you find these aliens and form an alliance with them. If you're right, you'll be going into space—who knows where or for how long. If you are wrong, well… let's not think about that."

"Yes, sir. Thank you, sir." Jones's chest swelled with pride for his friend. They were making the right decision.

The president scowled, looking pained. "Don't thank me. You do realize what you're up against, don't you?"

"Yes, sir."

"And not a word of this to anyone until you find these aliens. You don't know who is going to lose it or turn around and tell the press," the president insisted.

"Will do, sir. Shall we codename them the *out-of-town guests* then?"

"Sounds good. What do I tell the Joint Chiefs?"

"They've probably heard about the bodies and the wreckage already, so we should stick as close to the truth as we can. Perhaps a monkey-smuggling operation, but they were using a hydrogen weather balloon, which burned up in the crash."

"You think that would work?"

"Yes, smugglers are rarely concerned with safety. It'll appease them."

"So be it," the president said. "If you're wrong about the aliens…."

"If I'm wrong, history will judge me," Jones said, "but if I'm right, Earth may just survive, and that's all I care about."

The president turned to the window. "Let's just hope they're really the good guys."

CHAPTER FIVE

CHARLOTTE

ROSWELL, NEW MEXICO

Jones went to the local diner in town, and sat at a booth, reading the local paper. It had an article about the UFO on the front cover that made him concerned, but he believed in free speech. He knew that others in the government would discourage future articles and insist he change it, but he wasn't going to be the one to do it.

He felt tingles, so he lowered the paper to see a girl in a wheelchair looking straight at him. "Can I help you, little lady?"

She pushed herself over to him and sat up straight. Her dog sniffed him, wagged its tail and then sat. "Yes, hello. Are you the man in charge of the old warehouse?" She was wearing a press hat and acting older than her age, but Jones was impressed with her professionalism.

"And what do you know about that?"

"I know that the alien bodies and ship were taken there."

Jones knew it had to be a guess, but she was right. He smiled. "You seem to be well-informed, little lady. What's your name, and how did you come by this information?"

"I'm Charlie Baker from the *Roswell News*." She held out her hand for him to shake. "And you are?"

"General Jones." He leaned over to grasp her hand firmly, letting go as the waitress delivered a plate of steak and potatoes. "You are going to make an excellent reporter someday, Miss Baker. But for now, I would like to eat my meal while it is still hot."

CHAPTER SIX

MACHINE GUNS

OLD WAREHOUSE, NEW MEXICO

Jones was looking over the reports from the scientists when he heard machine guns. He quickly sprung from his seat, pulled his gun out, and ran to the bookshelves he had installed because they would absorb most bullets. Also, he liked to read.

He grabbed the radio and called the Roswell base for backup.

Then it was quiet for a while until he heard someone outside his door. He saw the knob turn, then two men crawled into his office. Jones pushed the door closed and cocked his gun.

"General Jones, sir?" a black soldier asked tentatively, as he slowly turned around.

"And you are?"

"Privates Malcolm Dow and Adam Rabinowitz, sir."

Jones felt tingles, so he knew they were OK, but continued his interrogation. "The two AWOL privates."

"With all due respect, sir, we were just trying to get a message to you," the other soldier said with a Jewish accent.

"What could be so urgent that you risk being court-martialed, and how did you get in here?"

"I arrived yesterday, but your guards tied me up and put me in a broom closet overnight."

"In a stolen jeep?" Jones asked.

Rabinowitz's face turned red. "Borrowed, sir."

"I arrived a short while ago to rescue him before they sent him to General Scornson," Dow explained. "Sorry about the machine gun sound effects."

"And I am to believe you, why?" Jones asked.

"Because the aliens want to meet with you, sir," Rabinowitz said.

Before Jones could say anything, they heard a knock at the door. Jones motioned with his gun for the two privates to hide behind the desk.

"Enter," Jones said. One of the gate guards came in, and again Jones closed the door, pushing his gun into the guard's back. "Yes?"

"Are you alright, sir?"

"I'm fine. What's all the noise about? Who's firing at us?"

"I don't know, sir. We couldn't find anyone or anything causing it."

That confirms their story. Jones smiled briefly. *If this is one of Scornson's men, he would be used to an angry and irrational response.* "You couldn't find it!?" Jones roared at the guard. "And you came in here empty-handed!?"

"Sorry, sir!" The guard's voice shook.

"I've called for backup, so try not to screw things up before they get here. Understood?"

"Yes, sir!"

"Get back out there and don't come back without results! Dismissed."

The guard took a quick look around the office before he left. After the door closed, Jones looked out the blinds and then decocked and holstered his gun. "You can come out now. It looks like you're telling the truth. He didn't report any intruders, and yet he was obviously looking to see if you were here. What made the gunshots?"

"A sound cannon from a spaceship, sir," Dow answered. "It projected the sound while causing the appropriate vibrations. It worked much better than I expected."

Jones raised a single eyebrow.

"What do we do now, sir?"

Jones circled to his side of the desk as Dow and Rabinowitz came out from behind it. Jones signaled them to sit as he did. "This location has been compromised. We go mobile, into the desert." He rubbed his chin. "They tied you up for trying to talk to me?"

"Yes, sir."

"Scornson and I have never seen eye to eye, but to plant spies on me? To order soldiers to attack one of their own? Who does he think he is?" Jones felt the blood pumping through his head. He was trying to think of what to do with Scornson when he remembered the aliens and his discussion with the president, and relaxed. "Never mind that now. Tell me about the aliens. If I remember correctly, you two were the first to discover the bodies."

Rabinowitz beamed. "Yes, sir! But those were just dummies, clones. When we went to pick up debris away from the crash site, we met one for real."

Jones cocked his eyebrow again. "Did you now? And those creatures were clones, hmm?"

"Yes, their ambassador said that they were grown in a lab, like plants."

"Fascinating. That would explain why the autopsy revealed no obvious cause of death, and why the doctor thought they were never born. I wish I could tell him that he's right! Alas, protocol." Jones stood and paced behind his desk. "Tell me more about them."

Dow and Rabinowitz locked eyes briefly. "They're pacifists, sir," Rabinowitz said.

"Pacifists, with advanced technology. The kind we wouldn't want our enemies to have, correct?"

Dow's eyes popped. "How did you know, sir?"

"I'm a Four-Star General, aren't I? Why else would they drop an obvious refugee decoy above the nuclear test site, but not steal anything?" Jones smirked. "They're obviously wanting our protection from whomever is attacking them."

Rabinowitz turned to Dow. "It looks like your hunch was correct."

Jones looked back and forth between the two of them. "Hunch?"

Dow closed his eyes and tilted his head to the ceiling.

"Yes, before we saw the alien, Dow sensed them, and then said they were friendly."

Someone else with hunches. "Very good." Jones waited for Dow to make eye contact, then smiled before continuing. "Now, what are they willing to give us in exchange for our help?"

Dow and Rabinowitz looked at each other. Rabinowitz answered. "Their technology, sir."

"What kind of weapons do they have?"

Dow frowned. "None, sir."

Jones stopped and stared at Dow.

"But they brought a married couple to teach us their advanced technology. They have tools that can be converted into weapons, but no weapons ready to go. Shame, too. I really wanted a ray gun."

"None? How could that be?"

"They didn't even have a word for weapons, sir. They want us and our weapons only as a backup plan, but it's our negotiators they're interested in," Dow said.

"Negotiators?" Jones looked back and forth between the two, trying to judge their expressions. "As long as they're willing to teach us their technology so we can defend Earth, I'm willing to help them in any way I can. How many of them are here?"

"On Earth? Six, sir. Do you think the president will agree, sir?"

Jones held back his laughter. "We already talked, and he wasn't impressed. I suspect he's more concerned with what the public would think if they found out he's dealing with aliens."

Dow nodded. "Yes, there is enough division between people already. Between blacks and whites…"

"…and Christians and Jews. Not that I'm a practicing Jew, I'm currently rebelling. You don't seem to be bothered by it, though. Why?" Rabinowitz asked.

Jones hummed. "What, you being a rebel and stealing a jeep? That does bother me, but we'll talk about that later." He chuckled. "But the division between people? I don't understand it. We're all people, blacks and whites, Christians and Jews, are we not?"

Memories of being a Junior Lieutenant came to mind. Being ordered to harass the young recruits who were *different*. While he respected them, he knew he *couldn't* change things by standing up for them now, and would only hurt his chances of being promoted.

Being forced to utter racial slurs, he wondered if they could see the sorrow in his eyes, or if they just heard the words from his mouth. After years of this, and several promotions, he was yelling at a subordinate and was about to use a racial slur, when he realized that he wasn't under orders to do it. He had risen to the point where he *could* make up his own mind and be the man that he once was. It would take time, but he *would* slowly change the system. He was in mid sentence when he left the soldier and found a quiet place to cry.

The memory left a lump in his throat, which he cleared before continuing. "I've lived long enough to know that it's not a person's appearance or religion that's important, it's their actions. Anyway, I asked the president whether he would rather deal with these aliens or with their enemies. That got his attention, and he reluctantly agreed to ally with them and put me in charge of this…" he looked at them intently, "… *Top Secret* project."

The two privates gave verbal confirmations.

"Good. Now, when am I going to meet these aliens?" Jones asked.

Rabinowitz pulled out a polished piece of metal about the size of a playing card. Jones looked on curiously. Rabinowitz smirked. "Connect us to Ambassador Geogram."

Jones looked at Rabinowitz's face. *He must be joking.* He looked down at the piece of metal in his hand. *That couldn't be some kind of communication device, could it?*

Dow was grinning. The bald head of a light purple being appeared on the metal.

Jones couldn't believe it. He expected advanced technology, sure, but this was far beyond anything he imagined. He remembered there were privates in the room, and hoped he didn't lose his composure.

"General Jones had it all figured out," Rabinowitz said.

The purple being crinkled his forehead, then nodded. *"Stimulating. Let me speak to him, please."*

Rabinowitz handed the device to Jones, who took a moment to admire it. "Fascinating!" He looked at Geogram. "General Frank Jones here. I understand that you are the ambassador for your people?"

"Yes. Ambassador Geogram, at your service."

"I can appreciate the precautions you took to protect yourselves. I can get you the help you need to defend your planet and negotiate, and I understand that you are prepared to teach us the technology to defend ours."

"Indeed, we are hoping to negotiate peace with our invaders, the people of Moad. What have Privates Dow and Rabinowitz shared with you?"

"They haven't shared much. I'm a military strategist, so I figured it out on my own. They just confirmed my suspicions. However, I do have one question left unanswered. How did you know that you could trust Privates Dow and Rabinowitz, as well as myself?"

"Our technology can detect such things as lying, fear, and hatred. We gave Private Rabinowitz a list of people who have worked with the debris that our technology has identified as 'safe'. He picked you to contact first."

Jones smiled at Rabinowitz. "A wise choice." Then he turned to Geogram. "I have already spoken with our president about helping you, and I have compiled a list of possible recruits for you and Corporal Dow to check out with this technology."

Dow jolted. *"Corporal* Dow?"

Jones chuckled to himself. He enjoyed making split-second decisions like this. "Yes. I'm promoting you two, and you will report directly to me. Dow, you are in charge of recruitment. Your first job is to test everyone on this base. We can't have anyone here who is afraid of aliens or isn't one hundred percent committed to working with them. Rabinowitz, you're my new clerk."

"Thank you, sir," Rabinowitz said.

"Thank you, sir, but you do realize that I'm black, sir?" Dow's eyes opened wide.

Rabinowitz let loose a laugh but quickly regained his composure.

"Exactly! And anyone who won't accept you is certainly not going to accept aliens. You can eliminate anyone who reacts negatively to you before you even open your mouth. If they pass that test, you ask them if they think aliens are friendly. If they pass that test as well, you tell them to report to me for a top-secret mission, which is the truth."

"Yes, sir…."

Jones turned to Geogram. "Ambassador—I think it's high time we meet face to face."

CHAPTER SEVEN

NEGOTIATIONS

ON A HOT DESERT HIGHWAY

"You want me to make an alliance with *aliens*? Did I hear that right?" Ryan Wilcox said.

Jones enjoyed throwing out shockers. He could have gently introduced the topic, but he's an army man, and testing a person's response was part of his job.

They were sitting in the back of a black stretched limo Jones had rented to make a good impression on the young man and his assistant, Donna Warren. Also, it had more room for the three of them.

Jones leaned forward, gaze steady. "Yes."

"You *must* be joking! How do I form an alliance with an alien race?"

Jones knew that Wilcox had been overlooked for too long. He had seen it many times and he couldn't understand why a good person was discouraged from doing what they do best.

But Jones saw it as his personal mission to bring out the best in people, to build them back up. "How did you negotiate the peace treaties?"

Wilcox cringed. "…I didn't. I gave my suggestions to the older and more competent men. They are the ones who negotiated the treaty!"

"I disagree. Yes, they did the negotiations, but they used your work. I'd say none are more competent than you, Wilcox. You are the son of one of the *best* ambassadors we have, but this requires a younger perspective." Jones smiled. "Your father tells me you've been negotiating since you learned how to talk. He says your mother could never say no to you about anything."

"I can vouch for that," Miss Warren said. "Well… since middle school, anyway. I helped him practice for the debate team. There wasn't an argument he couldn't win."

"Yes, but—"

Jones interrupted him. "You learned several foreign languages and cultures from your father's placements. You have a master's degree in politics." He paused. "Yes, you were a junior negotiator when you started, but you worked your way up, and the only things keeping you from being called senior negotiator are your babyface and your age."

Wilcox cringed.

"The president himself has noticed how hard you've worked, and the senior members of your team recommended you for an ambassador position when you're older."

Wilcox's eyebrows shot up. "They *did*? They didn't tell me that. —But that doesn't change anything! In Paris, I was one of many. Who do I have now?"

Miss Warren gave an exaggerated gasp. "*Um!*"

Wilcox barely glanced at her. He questioningly looked at Jones.

"In Paris, you were negotiating with multiple countries. Obviously, we can't bring in a lot of people on this. You've mentioned several times that you want an ambassadorship. This is the only way you are going to get one at your age. Your multicultural experience and love of space and science fiction makes you uniquely qualified for the job. The president and I thought you would *jump* at the chance." Jones sighed.

Wilcox turned pale. "I need more time to think it over. Is it possible for me and Donna to speak in private?"

"Sure," Jones said. He glanced over his shoulder through the divider window. "Corporal Dow, stop the car, please."

Dow eased the limo to the side of the road. The moment it stopped, Wilcox was out the door.

"Let's go for a walk," he said, holding the door for Miss Warren. Beyond seeing one of her feet leave the car, he didn't wait. He was already walking away at a quick pace. Jones watched as she grunted, trying to keep up with Wilcox.

"Where are they going?" Dow asked.

"Give him time. He'll come around." Jones was sure of it. He thought of himself as a good judge of character.

The two men made small talk while they watched Wilcox and Miss Warren walking and talking.

Dow looked at his watch. "How much longer? It's been almost half an hour!"

"It shouldn't be too much longer. Can you ask Geogram to standby to pick them up?"

Dow nodded. Then, almost on cue, Wilcox and Miss Warren turned around, and it looked like Wilcox was yelling something, but Jones couldn't hear.

Dow cupped his hands around his mouth in an attempt to be louder. "We are sending the alien ship to pick you up!"

A few seconds later, the couple disappeared.

Dow chuckled. "I would love to see their faces right now."

"Let's get in the car. Our friends will be here soon to pick us up."

Dow drove very slowly, and sure enough, in seconds they were on board the invisible spacecraft. Jones looked out the back window to see the landscape move. By the time Dow turned the vehicle around, the landscape stop moving. The tents, which make up their Area Two basecamp, were now in front of them. Dow drove slowly off the ship and parked.

Jones stepped out and saw Wilcox and Miss Warren standing and staring at him.

Jones smirked. "Did you enjoy your ride?" he asked as they approached.

"Was I…." Wilcox began, only for Miss Warren to glare at him. He coughed. "Um, sorry…. Were *we* just on a spaceship?"

"Yes," Jones said, "how did you like it?"

"Um, it's fast! I didn't have time to enjoy it."

Jones's smile widened. He was expecting something like that. "So, are you in or out?"

"I'm in."

"Good. You'll need this, *Ambassador* Wilcox." Jones offered the briefcase that was left in the car, then led them towards his office tent.

"Let's go talk before you meet with them. We thought you would be more comfortable negotiating on our home turf."

"*Home turf*? You mean *desert sand*." Wilcox laughed, and Jones and Miss Warren joined in.

Jones took them to his tent. It was plain, like any old military tent, with a foldout table in the middle, surrounded by four chairs, one of them occupied by Cpl. Rabinowitz looking at his communicator. Seeing Jones, Rabinowitz put the metal in his pocket, stood, and saluted. "General."

Jones returned the salute. "At ease. Corporal Rabinowitz, meet Ambassador Wilcox and Miss Warren."

They greeted each other and shook hands.

Jones joined Rabinowitz on the far side of the table. Wilcox and Miss Warren took the available seats. Wilcox popped open his briefcase and withdrew a notepad and several pens, which he set on the table between Miss Warren and himself. Jones slid a file across the table to Wilcox.

Jones gave them a few minutes to review the material before talking. "You should know a few things. First, the aliens are from a planet called Zalma, and we are calling them the Zalmen. They are pacifists, which means they know nothing about fighting. That also means they need all the help they can get against Moad—the planet that's attacking them."

He waited for Wilcox to nod before continuing. "In exchange for our help, they'll be giving us their technology and teaching us how to use it. Obviously, their technology is very advanced. They have no weapons, but I'm sure that our people can re-purpose their tools into weapons so we can defend Earth."

Wilcox looked up from the folder. "Not that I would imagine doing this, but what's stopping us from taking their technology and not helping them?"

"The same thing that tells me that you are not serious," Rabinowitz said. He tapped his glasses. "Zalmen technology can detect things like lying and hatred. They gave us these glasses to help us recruit people who are safe."

"Really? There is technology in those glasses?"

The three younger ones talked about the Zalma technology. Jones remembered asking about the communicator, and Geogram said that they could ask it to do anything and the device would either do it or tell him it couldn't. It had safeties so that it wouldn't do anything dangerous. That's all Jones needed to know. He'd already used it to call the corporals and the Zalmen a few times.

"Wait, wait...*change color*?" Wilcox's voice snapped Jones back to reality. He had been wondering about the colors.

"Yes, that's how they evolved into a peaceful society, or so he tells me," Rabinowitz said.

"How's that?"

"I don't know the specifics, but their color shows their emotional state. Red and yellow indicate anger. I think one of them blushed, so I am not sure what that means."

Wilcox leaned back in his seat, tapping his fingers on the table. "We turn red when we're angry or embarrassed, too. More blood flows to the skin, and it turns red, so, I would guess in both cases it is an emotional response, good or bad. But I don't know how the yellow fits in."

"And the greenish ones are scientists," Jones said, matter-of-factly. "They also become greener when they're thinking."

Wilcox frowned. "Thinking is not an emotion. And we saw a blue man on the ship. What does *blue* mean?"

"You said yellow indicates anger, correct?" Miss Warren asked, looking at Rabinowitz, who nodded. "Well, in the theater, when they want to create yellow lights, they mix red and green."

"So, angry means they're emotional, as indicated by the red; and thinking, as indicated by the green…." Wilcox said.

"How does that help us with *blue?*" Jones asked.

"Simple," Miss Warren said. "It's not there." She grinned, but Jones didn't get it.

After a brief pause, she continued, "when lighting, there are three primary colors: red, green, and blue."

"So, you're saying that when he is angry, he has no blue." Wilcox said.

"Possibly."

"So, blue might indicate tranquility, peace, or something like that?" Jones asked.

"It's possible. Why don't we just ask them?" Wilcox looked at Rabinowitz.

"I already did," Rabinowitz admitted. "They said it's not polite."

"Polite or not, it's my job to ask," Wilcox said. "What else do I need to know?"

Rabinowitz muttered into his communicator, then spun it around so that Wilcox and Miss Warren could see that the image changed to a video of a gleaming city. The sky above the city was filled with thundering explosions. "Their planet is protected by a deflector. We would like to have them here as well," Rabinowitz said.

Wilcox stared at the screen, eyes wide. He leaned back, looking up at Rabinowitz again. "What else?"

"Their invisibility?"

"And we don't want to store this technology on Earth," Jones added.

"What? Why not? Where would we store it then?" Wilcox asked.

"Their technology is beyond anything humans could dream of at this point. We don't want to risk it falling into the wrong hands. As for where to store it—we were thinking we'll be the only ones with spaceships, so we would like them to help us set up a base on the moon."

"So, you want me to negotiate a moon base? What could I offer them in exchange for all this?" Wilcox stood and began pacing the small tent.

Time for another shocker. "For one, you'll be going to their planet as a negotiator."

"I'm *what!?*"

"The president did inform you that you couldn't tell anyone where you were going, right?"

Wilcox cleared his throat. "Well, yes, but I expected it to be somewhere on Earth."

"I guess we should've discussed that first. Are you OK with traveling to their planet? They want to negotiate peace with the Moadites."

Wilcox leaned over his seat. "So now I'm not just negotiating with these pacifist aliens, I'm negotiating with their enemy as well!?"

Jones smiled. "Yes, but don't worry; I'm also going and bringing a team of military experts. You won't be on your own."

"Ah, so, we're trading manpower for technology?"

"Yes," Rabinowitz said. "They have brought instructors to teach us their technology. Their names are Kanara and Sarara, a married couple with two children. They're a swell family." He smiled.

"So, we are trading warriors and negotiators for teachers?" Wilcox addressed Jones. "What about this moon base? What are we giving them for that?" No one spoke. "Anybody?"

"I guess you're going to have to figure that one out," Jones said.

"*Great!*" Wilcox grumbled. "Any *more* good news?"

Jones hummed, thinking for a moment, then shook his head. "No, I think that's it. Are you ready to meet them now?"

"No!"

Jones chuckled to himself but maintained a poker face.

Wilcox sighed. "Oh, alright."

CHAPTER EIGHT

DOW MEETS CHARLIE

EARTH—ZALMA BASECAMP, NEW MEXICO

Dow came into Jones's tent panting. "General, someone is approaching the old warehouse." He handed his communicator to Jones. It displayed an image of a young girl in a wheelchair. Next to her was a golden retriever.

"That's the reporter girl, Miss Charlie Baker." Jones smiled. "Did you see the newsletter she printed?"

Dow shook his head.

"Shame. She's one smart cookie. She knew we had the crash debris at the warehouse, and she figured out we had Dr. Fisher in to perform an autopsy on the clones."

"Really, sir? How?"

"She has a keen eye for mystery. I'll look at what other information we have on her, but for now, I think I'll send you to talk to her. Keep an open com channel so I can listen in as well," Jones said. "I'll ask the Zalmen to take you there now."

"Yes, sir."

"And do you have that thing in your ear so I can talk to you, and she won't be able to hear?"

"Yes, I do."

"Excellent. Make it so."

Dow left the tent, then Jones asked Captain Agugua to fly Dow to the warehouse, and he agreed.

Jones appreciated the notebook size communicator the Zalmen gave him, it was easy to read. "Communicator, what information do you have on Miss Charlie Baker?"

It displayed the information her communicator had collected about her, such as personality traits; she was definitely dedicated to the truth. It listed other traits, and for some of the dramatic moments, such as when she went to the warehouse, it contained numbers, like heart rate, body temperature, etc. Jones was only concerned about the summary at the end.

Dow's voice came through the communicator. "*Sir. I've arrived at the warehouse, and am about to step off the Spacevan.*"

"Proceed." Jones heard the dog whine and bark twice.

After a brief pause, Jones heard, "*Hi, I'm Corporal Dow. I have orders to take the copies of the story you wrote.*"

"*No,*" Miss Baker's voice came through the communicator. "*That story is mine, and I won't let you cover* up the truth! Where did you come from, and where did everyone else go? This place is empty."

Jones smiled. *That girl has spunk!*

"*We can't stay in one place for long. Someone wrote a story about us being here, and there are bad people out there.*"

Jones appreciated how fast Dow came up with such a smart comeback.

"*Sorry about that….*" she said. "*A grumpy old soldier was asking about you. Is he one of the bad people?*"

"*I can't answer that.*"

"*You know you made a mistake with that weather balloon story.*"

That caught Jone's attention.

"*What mistake?*" Dow asked.

"*If you're working with aliens, you want the public to warm up to the idea,*" she said. "*Lying about it will just upset people.*"

She might have a point, Jones thought.

"*What makes you think that we're working with aliens? And if we were, why would we want the public to warm up to the idea?*"

"*I talked to General Jones a couple of days ago. He's a nice man. He's not the kind of person they would send in if they wanted to kill the aliens. Not like the guy who came into town today. And you want the public to warm up to the idea because you can't keep them secret forever. Once the public meets the aliens and finds out that you've* been hiding them, they won't be happy. You have to leave breadcrumbs."

Jones chuckled as quietly as he could to not disturb Dow.

"I'm going to ask you again for the copies of the story you wrote and all your notes."

"Or what?"

"Your dad knew or what. He did what he was told to do. The army can confiscate everything you have. They can discredit you so that you won't be able to get a job as a news reporter anywhere."

"My dad didn't have the information I have. I don't have much to confiscate, and I'm a girl. I can't get a job as a news reporter, anyway."

Jones chuckled. "She's brave, not afraid of aliens, but she was afraid of the guards that were there."

"You act brave, but I can see you are scared. Just like you were scared when you talked to the guards."

"I'm not scared, and I wasn't then, either."

"No, you are not scared of aliens, but you are afraid of the army."

"And how do you know?"

Jones remembered the data he had just read. "She has a communicator in her pocket that she picked up at the crash site."

"You took something from the ranch. Something that didn't belong to you," Dow said.

"I didn't take anything. What are you talking about?"

"Look familiar?" Jones guessed that Dow was show-ing his communicator.

"This? This is nothing. It was a scrap piece of foil when I found it. Hey…wait a minute. Are you telling me that you've been using this thing to spy on me?"

"It provided me with a summary of her personality," Jones supplied.

"In a manner of speaking, but it wasn't me, and spying is a strong word."

"Well, who then, and what word would you use?" Miss Baker demanded.

"Assessing…Interviewing…," Jones suggested.

"I can't tell you who, but I would say it was interviewing you," Dow said.

"Interview me? For what?"

"I have an idea. Let's hire her—an intern position, of course, due to her age. She has already proven her tenacity and wit. I believe she would be excel-lent for recording the facts of this momentous proj-ect," Jones said.

"General Jones was impressed with you. We don't have a lot of people who we can trust, but he told me he had a good feeling about you. If I told you the truth, could you keep it a secret?"

"I'm a reporter, that's not what I do."

"How about keeping it secret for now?" Dow amended.

"For now?" Jones asked Dow.

"How long?" she asked.

Jones chuckled. "You realize that could be decades, don't you?"

"Just until we deem it safe to reveal the truth to the wider world. So, what do you say, Miss Baker? Would you like to record history?" Dow asked.

"Record history? Excuse us for a minute. Sandy."

Who's she talking to? The dog? Jones thought.

"Tell me more."

"If she accepts, get a verbal contract from her to keep it secret," Jones told Dow. *"Communicator, can you record her promise, and play it back to her?"*

"Affirmative," it replied.

Dow also muttered an affirmative and focused back on the young reporter. *"Before we go further, I'll need a verbal contract that you won't go around sharing this information. I'm sure you know that."*

"And what if I promise but can't keep it a secret?" she asked in a challenging tone.

"She will be treated like all our other employees. Sharing top secret information, even by accident, would get her removed from the team," Jones said.

"If you tell anyone, then you'll be kicked off the team. No more recording history. No more learning about what really happened," Dow said.

Miss Baker was quiet for a long moment. Finally, she said. *"So, what you are saying is that if I can keep it secret, I can see what's happening and record it all? And one day I'll get to share it with the world?"*

"Yes."

"But how would this work? I'm still in school."

"I'll have an office building close to her home. She can tell her parents she is a research assistant," Jones said.

Dow repeated this to her, then she snarkily asked, "Aren't you worried about hiring a person in a wheelchair?"

"General Jones doesn't judge people on their appearance. He sees what a person can do, not what they can't."

Jones smiled.

"I wish more people were like him."

"So do I."

"Will I be interviewing people? Are they going to meet me there?" she asked.

Jones was going to reply, but Dow beat him to it. "We'll get the details sorted out later. Now, are you in? Can you keep a secret?"

"Yes, I can keep a secret. I'm in."

"Not so fast. We still need the verbal agreement. Take out that metal bar, hold it out like a mirror, say your name, and repeat our agreement."

"You're kidding me, right?" she asked.

Dow didn't answer.

"I, Charlie Baker, agree to keep the aliens a secret."

Jones heard the recording, then Dow chuckled. Jones wondered why and wished he had turned video on so he could see her reaction.

"What is it?"

"The aliens call it a communicator," Dow said.

"So you have been spying on me!"

"No one has been spying on you. The communicator just observed and only reported what it thought we needed to know and what it thought you wouldn't mind it telling us."

"What do you mean 'thought'? This tiny thing can think? And what did you need to know?" she asked.

"It told us that you are not afraid of aliens and you are a good reporter. Is there anything else we need to know?" Jones told Dow, and who repeated it.

"Is that all you told them?" she demanded of the communicator. She was silent for a few seconds, then…"How?"

"Alien technology, so don't show it to anyone. That's all you need to know for now. We will be in touch," Dow said.

"Alien technology? This little thing?"

The dog whined and barked twice.

"Corporal Dow?" she said.

"She can't see me. I'm back on board the Spacevan," Dow said. "Returning to base."

CHAPTER NINE

THE ALLIANCE

W ilcox entered Jones's tent.
Jones looked up from his paperwork. "Good morning, Ambassador. You've been in and out of meetings for the past two days. Have negotiations been going well with our guests?"

"Yes, sir." Wilcox lifted his briefcase onto the table. "They've been good, and we've signed the alliance." As he spoke, he opened the case and pulled out a stack of papers: copies of the alliance. He sat and slid them forward for Jones to see.

"Oh?" Jones reached for them.

"Well, sir. The Zalmen do have a sense of humor, but you have to explain the joke to them. The jokes they tell are very dry, but that's because they have little creativity. No imagination. No sense of adventure. No fiction."

"Interesting." Jones hummed thoughtfully. "How does that help us?"

"Well, you know that entertainment is a thriving industry. On Zalma, they have no means of creating it, which is why they were retransmitting our broadcasts. They want more—more books, records, and movies. Of course, the more violent content will have to have a warning, as they are pacifists. But it's the only physical thing that we have to trade with them."

"Fascinating. So, what are we trading with them for?"

"We give them one copy of all the music and stories that have been published in our country, and they give us a space base."

"A space base? Not a moon base?" Jones leaned forward, resting his elbows on the table.

"Edugra argued that if it's in space, it'll be closer to the planet, and it can be moved to help protect us. Like an aircraft carrier, but way bigger—and in space." Wilcox waved his hands, trying to illustrate the size.

Jones raised a single eyebrow. "Impressive."

"If we need anything else, we will have to get more stories from other countries in the United Nations to pay for them."

Jones tilted his head. "United Nations?"

"We'll get to that later."

"OK," Jones accepted, nodding. "What about the rest of the negotiations?"

"You know how our laws require us to bring treaties to the Senate?"

Jones nodded knowingly. "Yes, and we can't exactly do that, can we?"

"Not unless we want the whole planet to know about them and their technology. We have to do this off the books, out of the public's eye."

"Right, so what did you come up with?"

"The Earth–Zalma Alliance, or EZA for short, won't be written up as being with the US Government, but instead with the—" he made hasty air quotes "—'Peaceful Leaders of Earth'."

Jones's eyebrows shot up to his receding hairline again. "Oh boy! Is the president OK with this?"

"Surprisingly, yes. I think he just wants to share the burden with the other leaders," Wilcox said.

"I think you're right," Jones said. "How have you defined the Peaceful Leaders?"

"We have one year to form an Earth Defense Council and find the highest-ranking official in each country in the United Nations—safe people, of course. If we can't find a diplomat, we can recruit a military officer or a scientist. Regardless, each member should be given equal ranking on the council. Finding someone in the USSR might prove to be difficult."

"Yes," Jones said with a nod and a chuckle. "Corporals Dow and Rabinowitz have a real challenge on their hands."

"Yes, sir; they sure will. I almost forgot." He dug through his case again, this time to retrieve an envelope, which he presented with a stiff, formal posture. "I am here to officially notify you that the president has assigned you to lead a top-secret task force. Your assignment is to assemble the rest of the Earth Defense Council."

Jones shot him an incredulous look over the top of the letter. "Does the president know that I am going into space to fight aliens?"

"Yes, he does. You are to find someone to take over operations on Earth in your absence, and he is preparing a banquet for all the generals on Friday, so you and Dow can find your replacement."

Jones laughed, and jokingly he asked, "Is the president angry with me? He knows I don't like all this paperwork." He gestured to the table, with its stacks of official documents that needed reading and signing.

"I wouldn't say angry," Wilcox laughed along, "but he said that he doesn't want to be seen with aliens. It would not go well for him in the next election. And he mentioned that it probably would have been easier on all of us if you'd just fired a warning shot and scared them off. But he seems to respect you and what we're doing. He just won't admit it. And I'm sure he'll also take the credit if we're successful."

Jones chuckled. "Yes, I got that impression as well. What about our security problem?"

"The treaty states we will not keep their technology on Earth, except for a minimum required for recruitment purposes and self-defense."

"And what about our personnel exchange?"

"Right." Wilcox reached over the table to flip through the treaty; Jones scanned the newly revealed page. "Geogram will stay as the Zalma representative. Kanara, Sarara, and their children will stay to teach our scientists while you, your specialists, and I travel to their planet to negotiate and assess the situation."

"Good work!" Jones praised him. He folded the treaty together again, then leaned back and heaved a sigh. "Now, the hard part. I have to tell my wife that I'll be gone for two or three years."

"Good luck with that, sir."

Jones was in his office with Cpl. Dow. "Now, for the hard part. How to win this war without using violence?"

"Do you think that it is possible, sir?"

"I didn't think invisibility was possible, but..." Jones paused. "With technology that advanced, I don't see why we can't find a peaceful solution. But, as I said to the president, this technology is too advanced to let people know we have it. We can't let these Moadites know either, or they will want to negotiate or steal it. It will be a challenge. We will have to limit ourselves and match their technology level, and the technology that they know the Zalmen have, but I enjoy a challenge."

Dow nodded.

"But, in order to get the president's approval, I had to agree to travel to the alien planet. I am sure he thought that would deter me from this alliance, but I believe it is necessary. Just how do I tell my wife?"

Dow was silent.

"Geogram said it was a five-month journey in each direction, and it will most likely be longer. I don't want to worry my wife, but I don't want to give her false hopes either."

CHAPTER TEN

FIRST CALL TO ZALMA

BRIDGE OF THE SPACESHIP YMIT

"Ambassador Wilcox, meet Lieutenant Cameron and the Ymit's engineer, Joanua." Jones paused as Wilcox first shook the slender man's hand and then exchanged bows with the green engineer. "I've worked with Cameron for a long time. He is one of the best encryption specialists the army has to offer. While you've been negotiating, I've had Cameron learn their communications system from Joanua."

"A wise idea." Wilcox nodded toward Joanua. "Thank you." Then Wilcox turned to Cameron. "How did it go?"

"Great!" the lieutenant replied with a soft smile. "I had many ideas, and when you formalized the alliance, the ladies and I initiated implementation."

"So, what did you come up with?" Jones asked.

Cameron turned toward the main screens, which were lit up with multiple pages of code, in English. Jones realized it had to be for Cameron's sake.

"First," Cameron said, "we tested routing low-powered directional signals through their probes in other solar systems. That way, the Moadites should not be able to track the source."

"Smart," Wilcox said.

"Then I considered several of our encryption systems. The problem is that we can't transmit the encryption code to Zalma because anyone who intercepts it would also be able to decode our transmissions."

Jones shook his head, frowning. "And that's not good. So, what did you come up with?"

"We used a cipher key that only both sides have without transmitting. Since they have all their manuals and historical books electronically stored on the ship's computer, we coded a multibook cipher," Cameron explained.

"Multi-book!" Jones repeated. "Impressive!"

"Thank you, sir," the lieutenant said before he continued his explanation. He used his hands minimally as he spoke. "Once they have that, we will immediately send a secure transmission with more encryption algorithms. And, for really secure transmissions, the Zalmen can enter additional personal keys, like: *Where did we first meet?* With the Zalma super-fast computers, multi-layered secure communications are possible, and I am confident that the signals are secure."

"Wow!" Wilcox said.

Cameron smiled. "The Zalmen are excited, as they haven't contacted their leaders and family since they left."

"Oh?" Jones glanced around at the collected aliens.

"Yes," Wilcox said. "They told me that they sent brief automated messages that would look like one of their probes so the Moadites wouldn't pay any extra attention."

Jones hummed. "Good plan."

"With your and Captain Agugua's permission, sir, we are ready to start," Cameron said. When they both nodded, he and Joanua began uploading their files.

"The first probe has updated," Edugra said. "Second…. Third…. Fourth…. Fifth…. Sixth…. The seventh and final probe is now updated. We are transmitting encryption programs and terms of our alliance to Zalma," Edugra finished.

For the next few seconds, no one spoke. They waited with bated breath. Then the computer chimed, and a new rectangle popped up.

Edugra smiled. "Incoming coded transmission from Zalma!" she announced.

Everyone cheered. The humans exchanged hand-shakes. Edugra accepted the transmission. Sarara even clapped her hands together. The text vanished from the screen, and a live video transmission appeared.

Several Zalmen stared back at them through the screen with an assortment of blue, purple, and teal skin. All but one was dressed in silver robes.

Agugua bowed and spoke first—in Zalmen, which his communicator then translated to English for the humans. *"Council, I would like you to meet Ambassador Wilcox, General Jones, and Lieutenant Cameron."* He pointed to each of them in turn. *"They are responsible for enabling us to communicate today."*

Jones bowed to the people on the screen in time with Wilcox and Cameron. He'd been distracted by studying the Zalman in the middle, the only one he'd ever seen wearing a different color. He wore a robe like the rest of the council, though his was a glossy white. He appeared to be Geogram's age, in his late fifties by human standards, though, unlike the ambassador, this Zalman was a much darker purple.

"I am First Minister Ronderra."

Jones immediately noticed that his words didn't match the movement of his lips. When Agugua spoke, the computer translated, so Jones wasn't too surprised.

Ronderra continued, *"Thank you, gentlemen. We are grateful for your assistance. The deflectors are less effective than when our team left, and our timeline has been moved up. We believe the Moadites have new technology."*

As he spoke, a secondary image popped up, showing video footage of the planet's deflectors under enemy fire. One explosion, larger and brighter than any of the others, lit up across the screen. The entire Zalman sky flickered, casting spectral lights over the city buildings. Many of the Zalmen gasped, then breathed a sigh of relief when they saw what looked like the glass of a snow-globe rebuilding itself.

"We are glad to be of service," Jones said. "I'll be returning with your outreach team and with a small group of specialists to assess your needs."

Geogram stepped forward, bowing to the first minister. "I can vouch for General Jones's skill. He deduced our intentions from our decoy ship and its proximity to their nuclear test site. He and his team will be invaluable to us."

On the screen, the council members' colors flickered, and they murmured, clearly impressed.

"The best course of action for now would be to begin analyzing the Moadite ships," Jones continued. "We need to know what they're made of, and if they have deflectors. Would you be able to do that?"

"*Yes, that is possible,*" Ronderra replied.

"Analyze their weapons as well," the general persisted. "I'd suggest launching rocks or metal debris into space and scanning the remains after they've been destroyed. If we can identify what types of weapons they're using, we might be able to modify your deflectors for better resistance."

The first minister's face flickered with green, then he nodded.

"Finally, we'd like you to record their ships' transmissions for us, so that we can have our decryption specialists take a look at them," Jones finished.

"We will do as you request," the first minister assured him.

One of the teal council members lifted a large communicator into view, taking the moment of silence as her cue to step forward. *"We are pleased with the success of the mission,"* she said first, then stared down at her communicator again. *"I see here that in exchange for human goods, we will be providing a station for your orbit."*

She looked up for confirmation, and Jones nodded. *"We have been preparing an invisible freighter for our new colony, but I believe our chances would be better if you use it as your space station. It has a large replicator and everything needed to start a space fleet."*

"Thank you." Jones acknowledged. He paused for a moment, then asked, "New colony?"

"Yes. In light of our weakening deflectors, we have been preparing to evacuate the planet." She'd barely gotten the words out before gasps erupted from the Ymit's crew members.

In his peripheral vision, Jones noticed the crew member skin colors fluctuating aggressively.

Jones spoke slower, with a deeper voice. "I'm sorry to hear that. I assure you we are doing everything we can to eliminate the need for evacuation."

"We had planned to use this ship as the base for our new colony," the teal council member maintained, *"but with your help, we hope we will not need it."*

"We look forward to these books and movies you are sending," a third Zalman added, *"both historical and artificial. They will be a welcome distraction to our people during these difficult times."* He gave a halfhearted smile.

Cameron and Wilcox were muttering.

"Well," Jones said, sending a quick frown in the two men's direction, "I am sure you have lots to talk about. We will leave you to it."

The three humans bowed and left.

CHAPTER ELEVEN

MRS. JONES

JONES FAMILY HOME

Jones shuffled into his house. There was a lump in his throat. "Chloe…. Honey…um…."

Chloe put her hands on her hips. "Francis Jones! You are going away again, aren't you?"

"You know me too well." Jones was relieved not having to say it.

"I would ask where, but I know better. You can't tell me. How long this time?"

Jones looked down. "At least a year."

Chloe spat out words in French, as she always did when upset. "A year? I was expecting the usual three months." She sighed. "But, I guess they need your strategic mind, and I'm afraid there is no one better."

The tension in his muscles relaxed. He held her in a warm embrace as he played on her words. "Don't be afraid, my dear." Jones tried to lighten the mood. "I'm going with the best technology and team there is. I picked them all myself."

"I'm not actually afraid. I know our president wouldn't send you to any place dangerous. He doesn't want to lose you any more than I do. Do we have time to tell the kids?"

"Yes, invite them to dinner next weekend. Oh, and I have something for you." He pulled a box out of his jacket pocket.

Chloe opened it. Inside was a locket with his and her pictures in it. "It's wonderful!"

"Now, you won't be alone. Anytime you need me, you can see me and talk to me." Jones was being deceivingly honest. While it was a normal photo, the metal was a communicator. Anytime she opened it, it would record her voice and, as a communicator, decide if it should send the recording to him or call locally for help.

He didn't want to spy on her, and he didn't want the temptation to talk back to her, so there was no camera, screen, or speaker, just a one-way transmitter. They were also setting up a spaceship-to-shore phone line if they needed it.

She closed the locket and gave him a kiss and a hug. "I'll miss you."

CHAPTER TWELVE

BLUE MONDAY

EARTH–ZALMA BASECAMP, NEW MEXICO

Jones had been discussing possible new recruits with Cpl. Dow, but he looked up and saw Wilcox's face was pale.

"Ambassador." *What can I say to calm his nerves?* "I hear things didn't go well on the weekend while I was away."

Wilcox heaved a sigh, his face downcast. "No general, they did not! I goofed. Did you know that they're vegetarians? I mean, we should have guessed with the whole pacifist thing. They can't kill an animal to save their life, literally!"

"Oh, that is a problem," Jones said. "I like my steak!"

"They called us barbaric and kicked us off the ship, then threw our luggage outside. I went back this morning to see if they were still there, but the door was closed. It's so weird. I can feel the doorway, but the rest of the ship isn't there. It's like they flew away without it!"

"The first time I entered the ship, they told me that it was in another dimension or something so it couldn't be detected, but they kept the door partially in our world so we can go in and out," Dow said.

"Is that even possible?" The question was rhetorical, but both young men shrugged anyway, and Jones sighed. "Is there any *good* news?"

"Yes," Wilcox replied. "Donna has been talking to Edugra on her communicator. They've built up a friendship."

Get to the point man! "And?"

"Donna prefers vegetarian food; she only eats meat when the people around her are. She has been sympathizing with them." Jones was growing impatient. "It turns out that all animals on Zalma are vegetarian. Sure, they eat eggs and drink milk, but no animal on their planet kills another. No animal eats another. They had no concept of what meat was."

"Well, now. I can see why they were so upset. That must have been quite a shock. What are you going to do about it?"

"What can I do?" Wilcox asked. His tone bordered dangerously on a whine. "They're not answering my calls, and I already told you the door's been closed since they kicked us out on Friday."

Dow chuckled. "How's that for timing?" he asked. "It's opening now."

The others turned to him. He hadn't moved, but he was looking at the side of the tent with interest.

"Zalma technology," the corporal explained, pointing at his glasses. "I can see heat through thin material—mostly a person's body heat. Someone is exiting the ship. Benjamin identifies him as Geogram, and he is heading this way."

"Benjamin?" Wilcox asked.

"That's what I decided to name my communicator," he replied.

Just then, Geogram entered the tent. He had a stiff posture and cold eyes. "Greetings. At the request of my daughter Edugra, I am inviting Ambassador Wilcox and Miss Warren back to the ship to talk. But there will be no—" he cleared his throat "—*dead animals* on board! Is that understood?"

Jones felt pride in how Geogram spoke with authority and replied instinctively. "Yes, sir."

Geogram was taken aback but seemed pleasantly surprised with the response.

"Good. Ambassador, please retrieve your assistant so we may continue our discussions." Geogram headed back to the spaceship.

Jones had called a meeting with the whole team. When Wilcox came, Jones introduced him to the men.

"We've recently learned that there are no carnivores on Zalma. None whatsoever on the whole planet." Wilcox paused, but the men were silent. "That means they've never heard of one animal eating another. They were horrified to hear that we do it all the time."

"What that means for *us*," Jones said, stepping in, "is that they won't allow us to bring meat onto the ship."

A chorus of groans rose from the assembled men, though none voiced complaints yet, so Wilcox forged ahead.

"I am sorry, I have been trying to negotiate a compromise…but the Zalmen are strict vegetarians and *very* set in their beliefs. I'm afraid the ladies might spew if I even bring up the topic when they're around."

Sergeant Bruno Abbott, a soldier in mind and body, stood first. "If that's the case, I'm not going!" he declared. "No meat, no marine! The president isn't ordering us out…right, general?"

"Correct." *I hate to admit it, but…* "This is a voluntary mission."

"This is the chance of a lifetime. Think of the technology we will gain," Wilcox interjected.

Abbott spat into the dirt. "I don't care about technology. I'm a soldier! I say you're just whistlin' dixie with these chromedome aliens. Oddballs, all of them. Who doesn't eat *meat*?"

Brian Howard, a civilian weapons designer, spoke up. "Well, I *am* interested in their technology. I could try going vegetarian, but I don't know how long I would last."

"The good news is that they have expanded their garden so we can have our fresh fruit and vegetables, and they are willing to make room for the general's personal chef."

"That'd be better than any field ration kit, but…he can only cook vegetarian?" asked Lieutenant Colin McKenzie, a pilot.

More protests arose from the group, but Jones lifted a hand, and they all fell silent. "Wilcox, you've got one day to work things out, or the president's likely to pull the plug on this whole thing, and you know he'll do it. He's been clear in his opinion of this from the start. Dismissed!"

Gen. Jones summoned the ambassador team to his tent. He knew this was Wilcox's worst scenario come true. The alliance had failed. "You did an incredible job," he said, trying to comfort them.

Wilcox looked away. "Thank you, sir. I just—"

"It was *not* your fault, son," Jones said firmly, cutting off his protests. "You did everything you could." *What does he need to hear from me?* "The president and I want you to know that we are very proud of you."

"Thank you, sir."

Miss Warren leaned over the back of Wilcox's chair before settling in the one next to him. She, too, looked forlorn. "It would've been sweet to go into space, but I guess it wasn't in the cards. How did we even start working with aliens in the first place? I doubt they flew right up to the White House to talk to the president."

Cpl. Dow grinned cheekily at Cpl. Rabinowitz. "I was the first human to meet them, actually."

"How'd that happen?" She stared at the corporal with wide, curious eyes. The corners of her lips were upturned with interest.

Rabinowitz spoke before Dow got a chance. "Our detachment was called in to clean up a crash site near Roswell."

I love these two clowns.

Dow cut in. "They thought it was a supply container or something, but it was a spaceship, like a lifeboat. Inside, we saw three dead aliens."

Wilcox frowned. "You never mentioned anything about *dead* aliens before."

Dow chuckled. "Oh, the aliens in the ship were dummies. They wanted to test our reactions."

This time Rabinowitz cut in. "After that, we met the *real* alien, Geogram. He asked for our help to contact the government, and from there, I sought out General Jones."

"Yes. I was the commander of the base and was called to inspect the wreckage. The proximity to the nuclear test site had me concerned, until I realized that it looked more like a refugee situation than a military one. When Dow and Rabinowitz showed up, they confirmed my suspicions."

Wilcox raised his eyebrows. "So, how'd you figure it out? Was it because the dummies were fake?"

Jones shook his head. "No, they were quite real. I had the local veterinarian do an autopsy on the alien bodies, and the doctor said that while he had never seen anything like them, their bodies reminded him of a stillborn calf."

Rabinowitz nodded. "Geogram told us that they're genetically modified clones."

"Cloning?" Miss Warren repeated, disbelieving. "As in the novel, *A Brave New World*? Creating two identical beings?"

"Yeah, that's it. You read it too?"

"They were very convincing clones," Jones explained. "The doctor who performed the autopsies believed they were real, but he didn't know how they died."

"Did you ever find out?" she asked.

"They were never alive," Dow explained. "They were grown in a lab like plants."

Wilcox's eyes widened. "*Wait?* They just grew a *body?*" He paused. "What if they could grow other animals, like a cow?"

Jones's heart pounded. He felt flushed. "Oh my God! How did we miss this? Do you think it would work?"

"Do you think *what* would work?" Dow asked, staring between both of them in confusion. "What are you talking about? Did I miss something?"

Wilcox turned to him. "The Zalmen are against us *killing* animals to eat them. But they eat eggs, which are also animals, just that they were never alive to begin with. Would they still be against us eating meat if it was never alive either?"

Jones, Dow, and Rabinowitz stood outside at the edge of camp, staring up at the cloudless sky hoping for the alien ship to return.

Jones heard footsteps behind him. They definitely were too light to be soldiers; they must be the ambassador team. "So, what did they say?" he said without turning.

"Geogram doesn't see a problem with us eating cloned meat on board the ship. He suspects that the council will stipulate that you do not eat meat in public on Zalma, or discuss meat with any Zalmen. He's concerned that if their people saw meat, even cloned, they would wonder what it is, and the answer would cause the same fear that they experienced at our first meal, and he doesn't want his people to be afraid of us. He told me he'd discuss it with their council and see if they felt the same. Then, he'll let us know," Wilcox said.

Dow nodded, then turned away from the sky and rubbed at his eyes.

"Care to finish your stories?" Miss Warren asked.

Jones and the two corporals took turns telling their stories. When they were finished, they looked up.

"I don't know why we are looking!" Dow protested. "I have never seen their ship; it's always invisible. Have any of you seen it?" He looked at the others.

Everyone shook their heads.

After a few hours, Dow sighed. "Well, I guess they're not coming back," he said. "You'd think that they could have at least called." With a huff, he hauled himself up off the ground where he'd been lying and was just about to head back to his own tent for the night when something finally changed.

A song was playing, coming from an unseen source. There was something shining in the sky. At first, it looked like a star, but it was getting bigger. The song was growing louder.

The star was soon too big to be a star, and Jones saw the Ymit for the first time. It was a massive flying rectangle, descending from the darkening sky. The outside gleamed silver, reflective, and shiny.

"How does that thing even fly? It doesn't look aerodynamic whatsoever," Wilcox said.

"If they can make it invisible, control gravity, and grow clones, I think they can make a shoebox fly," Dow replied.

"'You Are My Sunshine'!" Miss Warren shouted excitedly. "That's Ryan's and my favorite song!"

"Wow, it's huge!" Dow shouted.

When the song finished small projectiles shot out from the ship and into the sky, exploding in a burst of sparks and color. Pops and bangs filled the air, jolting the entire basecamp of Area Three.

A dozen other recruits ran out of their tents, some holding their rifles, ready to fight off the invading forces, but then they looked up, and their jaws dropped.

As the first round of fireworks cleared, another song played, this time, smooth jazz.

Jones hummed. "'Sentimental Journey'. That's *my* favorite." He was pleased. "And would you look at that display! They must be learning imagination." Then he chuckled, looking around at the looks of awe on the soldiers' and civilians' faces. "It's a good thing we're the only ones around for miles out here in the desert."

A second round of fireworks began. It opened with a shower of gold, then stars of blue and red. The sky, once painted by the sunset, was awash with more colors. After the fireworks were over, a third song, an upbeat tune on a trumpet, began to play.

"'Boogie Woogie Bugle Boy'," Dow identified. "That's the one *I* told Joanua about."

They listened with wide grins on their faces, and as the song ended, a third display of lights filled the night sky around the hovering ship. Then it descended the rest of the way and touched down on the empty desert. A door opened, and in the distance the aliens came out and were walking toward them. "That was quite an entrance!" Wilcox called as they got closer.

Geogram nodded politely, sending a quick smile at his daughter. "We observed your Fourth of July celebrations before we sent the decoy and based it on that. Did we get it right?"

Wilcox grinned. "Yes, I'd say so!"

CHAPTER THIRTEEN

THE BANQUET

WASHINGTON, D.C.

The president's banquet had finally arrived, and Jones was slowly making his way through their list of potential replacements for when he left for Zalma. One of the younger generals, a man of about forty-five, caught Jones's eye. He approached. "You're Newman, aren't you?" he asked.

"Yes, sir. General Jones, I've followed your career, and I must say, I've always been so impressed."

"Thank you," Jones said. *A suck-up, is he? Well, we'll just have to change that.* He turned slightly and swept his arm out. "This is my recruitment clerk, Corporal Dow."

The corporal saluted.

Newman returned the salute. "Corporal Dow."

"Nice to meet you, General Newman," Dow replied.

"Now that the pleasantries are out of the way," Jones said, nodding sharply before facing Newman again, "have you heard that I am heading a new project down in New Mexico?"

"I believe so, yes. A weather balloon crashed in Roswell, correct?" he asked, and Jones nodded again. "What really happened? Did you catch an enemy spy? Or should I believe the papers about the aliens?" he joked.

So, he doesn't believe in aliens. This should be interesting. "Which would you prefer?"

"Umm…. Either one is fine with me, sir."

He's just saying what he thinks I want to hear. I hate when they do that, but I love the challenge. "If you were in charge, how would you approach the situation?"

"I would assess their intentions, sir," he said. "I'd interrogate if hostile, debrief if friendly."

"So, you are saying you would treat an alien and a spy the same way? If they are friendly or hostile, treat them as such?"

"Yes, sir. If a spy is defecting, you are more likely to get information from him by treating him with respect."

I can't read him. If he doesn't believe in aliens, will he be afraid of them when he meets one? Jones looked at Dow, who was using his Zalmen glasses to test Newman. After a few seconds, Dow turned and nodded to Jones.

"Good answer," he said. Then, completely changing the topic, he asked, "Do you play chess?"

"O-of course, sir. Yes."

"Would you like to play a game next week?"

"Yes, sir. It would be an honor, sir."

"Good, good. I'll have Corporal Dow contact your office."

"Thank you, sir," Newman said.

"Excuse us, we have more people to speak to." Jones and Dow walked away, but they didn't get far before they ran into Gen. Scornson and Sgt. Lawless, who Dow exchanged heated glances with.

Scornson and Lawless headed straight for Newman. Jones tracked their movements from the corner of his eye.

As soon as Jones and Dow had met everyone on their list, they found a quiet corner to talk.

"What's your assessment?" Jones asked.

"The Zalmen technology worked," Dow replied. "I could see most generals' heart rates accelerate and temperatures increase the moment they saw me approach with you. Newman shows the most promise, but..." His expression pinched.

"Yes, he has no moral compass; he's not ready yet. However, Scornson might be just what he needs."

"How so, sir?"

Jones looked down, and he felt a lump in his throat. "Scornson will try to get to us through Newman, who will then have to pick a side. It won't be easy for him, but I'm sure he will pick ours."

CHAPTER FOURTEEN

CHESS

NEWMAN'S OFFICE

"Welcome, General Jones," Newman said as the older general entered. He rose to shake the other man's hand; they exchanged pleasantries, then they sat face to face at his desk. Jones looked down at the board thoughtfully. Newman gave him the white pieces, and therefore, the first move.

Wanting to test Newman and give him a fair chance, Jones turned the board so their pieces were switched, and motioned for Newman to go first.

Newman raised an eyebrow, then moved his first pawn to E4.

"I saw you speaking with General Scornson at the banquet." *I'll give him a false sense of security.* He moved one of his pawns to D5. "Was there anything particularly interesting that you discussed?"

"Just the usual pleasantries," Newman replied then took Jones's pawn.

"I see. Did you notice that Scornson talked to everyone Dow and I talked to?" This was Jones's way of warning Newman. Then Jones took his pawn.

Newman moved his next pawn to D4, then Jones returned his queen to its initial square. "No, I didn't."

They made several moves before Jones asked, "Do you remember our conversation at the banquet?"

"Our conversation? The one about spies and aliens, sir?"

"Do you remember what you said to me?"

"I said I would treat them the same, sir. I'd assess whether they were hostile or friendly, and I'd treat them as such. But sir, what do you mean exactly when you say *aliens*? Do you mean foreigners, or beings from outer space?"

This should be interesting. "Does it matter to you where someone comes from?" Jones leaned back in his chair and folded his arms.

Newman looked back at the board and made another move. "Well, no, but I don't believe in aliens from outer space. Respectfully, sir."

"But if they were real?" Jones was completely calm as he pushed his queen forward. With a knight and bishop flanking it.

"What do they look like? Do they speak English?"

Jones smiled. *He's finally considering that aliens might be real.* "Let's pretend, for our hypothetical situation, that they appear human, just their skin's a different color than ours. And yes, they do speak English."

"OK, then I would assess their mental state and their motivation. If they're coming from space…. Are they invaders?"

"Let's say you've conducted your assessment, and the aliens seem mentally stable. They are not invaders. In fact, they have a mutually beneficial proposal."

Newman's eyebrows nearly shot off his face. "If that's the case…I guess I would cautiously proceed with it and see where it leads."

Jones was pleased. *Now it's time to test his teamwork skills.* "I hear that you've just wrapped up an important mission. How did it go?"

Newman leaned back and formed a triangle with his fingers. "I caught the traitor, so I'd say it was a success."

Jones knew that much. "And to what do you owe that success?"

"I laid out the bait and followed the one who took it."

I know that he likes to work on his own, however, that will have to change. "What about your team?"

Newman shrugged. "They were helpful."

Oh, come on man…. "Who specifically was helpful to you?"

Newman clenched his jaw. "Specifically? No names come to mind."

Jones chuckled. "You're not much of a team player, are you?"

"O-of course I am, it's just…," Newman began, but the protests died on his lips. "I work well with my superiors."

"That's what I thought. You don't pay much attention to the little guys, do you?" To emphasize his point, he captured Newman's last pawn right across from Newman's king. "Checkmate."

Newman's eyes were wide as he scanned the board over and over again.

"You show promise, but you're too busy trying to get ahead. You don't see what's right in front of you," Jones told him then stood. "That was enjoyable. Thank you for the game. How about another tomorrow? Same time?"

Newman dragged his eyes away from the board. "Yes, sir. Thank you, sir."

When Jones arrived the next day, he noticed Newman was watching him closely. *I see his talk with Scornson went as expected.*

Once again, he'd set up the board with white pieces on Jones's side, and this time Jones accepted. He took the first move, pushing one of his pawns forward two spaces. And so, the game began.

Several moves in, Jones finally spoke. "Newman. I'm excited to see what you've learned since our last game."

"Yes, sir."

Newman made another play, capturing the general's rook with a knight. The motion placed Jones's king in check.

"Hmm…good move." Not for long, though. Jones easily countered, capturing Newman's knight. "So, continuing our hypothetical discussion from yesterday, if you met face-to-face with an alien, what would you do?"

"Can you be more specific? What country are they from?"

Jones smiled, knowing that Newman was playing dumb. "Do you still believe that there are no aliens out there?"

Newman tilted his head and looked up. "Mathematically, the odds that there *isn't* life out there are pretty small, but the technology needed to travel between planets…. I don't believe anyone is capable of that yet. Maybe in a couple of decades."

"They can't have that technology?"

"With all due respect, sir, we humans don't have those capabilities, so I'm having a hard time believing that any alien could either. I have faith in our country's—our planet's—scientists."

"So, it's possible for aliens to be out there, but they can't be more advanced than us. Is that what you're saying?" Jones pressed, leaning forward slightly as he sliced his queen across the board.

Newman stared down at the queen. "Yes.... No...." He mumbled a few words under his breath. "I'm not sure, sir."

Finally! Jones chuckled. "That's probably the most honest answer you have given me."

Newman's shoulders sagged in defeat.

"You're trying to give me the answers you think that I want to hear, but what I want from you is the truth."

"Yes, sir. Sorry, sir." His shoulders hunched, but then he straightened his posture and made another move in the game and captured another pawn.

For the next ten minutes, the only sound in the office was the soft click of the game pieces on the polished board.

His skills are getting better. I wonder if he will recognize this move? Jones moved his piece and Newman moved to counter it.

Jones hummed his appreciation. "You're getting better. But you still have much to learn," he complimented as he captured Newman's bishop, nonetheless. Then, switching the topic entirely, he asked, "Who do you think our biggest enemy is?"

"Haven't we defeated all our enemies, sir?"

"What about the enemy within?"

Jones was talking about the battle he knew Newman was going through right now. Would he choose to believe Scornson or him. Newman pulled his arms in tightly, and remained quiet.

"I see we've gone into unfounded territory. I apologize. Why don't you tell me more about your family? Where did you grow up?"

"Colorado," Newman replied, "but my father was in the army too, so we moved around quite a bit and ended up in Washington, D.C."

"I'm sure you're making your father proud. You're quite accomplished for your age." Newman made a slight scoff, and Jones raised an eyebrow. "Now I'm getting the feeling he doesn't feel that way. How come?"

Newman stiffened at the comment.

His eyes are shifting back and forth. He is fighting his childhood demons. There is no point in continuing the game. "Checkmate."

Newman's eyes popped as he checked the board.

Jones forged on, not even allowing Newman to reply. "Thank you for the game. You're much improved, but as I said, you still have a way to go."

"Thank you, sir."

Time to drop another shocker. "I'd like you to come see my operation."

"It would be an honor, sir."

"Good." Jones stood and shook Newman's hand, then retrieved his coat and hat from the rack. He opened the door. "I'll have Corporal Dow make the arrangements with your assistant for next week. Another game tomorrow?"

Newman nodded, and Jones left.

Jones was busy and didn't see the point in playing another game of chess, so he sent Corporal's Dow and Rabinowitz to test Newman. Their experiences with Lawless and Scornson should be enough to convince him to do the right thing.

Jones's notebook-sized communicator buzzed.

"Answer," he said to it.

An image of Dow appeared with Newman and Rabinowitz behind him.

"What is that thing?" Newman demanded.

Dow didn't answer him. *"Sir, you were right. Scornson has been blackmailing General Newman."*

"And?"

Rabinowitz stepped toward the device. *"General Scornson sent a briefcase with a tracker. We could disable the tracker, but that would alert Scornson to our knowledge and put General Newman in harm's way."*

"We don't want Scornson to know that we know. Redirect him instead."

"Yes, sir." Dow saluted sharply, and the screen went blank.

Jones and the corporals knew the communicators were made of nanites, and could do practically anything, so the plan was to leave one, and then remotely tell it what to do.

But not too soon. Scornson could check on the brief-case during the weekend. When the men returned, they would consult with the Zalmen and determine what action to take and when.

CHAPTER FIFTEEN

THE JONES FAMILY DINNER

JONES FAMILY HOME

Jones sat at the head of the table, surrounded by his family. He smiled as he looked around at his children, their spouses, and his grandchildren. He had never felt so proud, yet so heartbroken.

"So, Dad, what's this big mission you're going on?" asked his eldest son, Pierre.

Jones hesitated before responding, "It's a top secret operation. I'm afraid I can't say much about it."

"But it's important, right?" asked Bethany.

"Yes, it is," Jones said, his voice heavy with emotion. *If I don't succeed, we won't have a way to defend you from aliens.* "It's an opportunity to make a real difference…."

Jones didn't know how to end the sentence: *in the world* or *in the galaxy*? But it didn't matter, as he was broken out of his thoughts by Claire, his youngest daughter.

"But what about us?" she asked. "Are you sure you have to go? Can't someone else do it?"

"I wish I could tell you more, but it's something I have to do," Jones said, regret shooting through his gut.

"We understand, Dad," Charity said. "We're proud of you, but we're going to miss you."

As they ate dinner, Jones couldn't shake the feeling of guilt. He wanted to be honest with his family, but he couldn't risk telling them about the aliens. After dinner, he helped Chloe with the dishes, trying to put on a brave face.

"Is everything OK, Frank?" Chloe asked, sensing that something was off.

Jones let out a sigh. "It's just hard, leaving you and the kids behind. And not being able to tell you everything about the mission."

"I know," Chloe said, wrapping her arms around him. "But we'll be here waiting for you when you come back. And we'll always be proud of you, no matter what."

Jones held Chloe tightly, knowing that this could be the last time they were together. He was filled with a mix of sadness and determination. He knew he had to go, but it was going to be the hardest thing he had ever done.

CHAPTER SIXTEEN

INTERVIEW

ROSWELL OFFICE

Jones opened the back door and stepped out of the Spacevan.

The dog whined and then barked twice. Miss Dianne stood and saluted, so Miss Baker did as well.

Jones chuckled, then returned the salute to Miss Dianne. "As you were." Turning to Miss Baker, he said, "Civilians don't have to salute. Miss Dianne may be dressed in regular clothing, but that's because she is undercover."

Baker turned to Dianne with a big smile. "You're a spy?"

"I never thought of it that way. I'm just a plain-clothed contact person."

Jones smiled. "Shall we begin?" He and Baker entered the office with the desk.

Baker pulled her communicator from her pocket and set it up. *"Watson, record."*

Jones looked at his watch. *How much time do I have for this?* "I have a very long flight to catch, so let's get on with it."

"May I ask where you are flying to?"

"Zalma," Jones said without hesitation.

Her eyes popped. "Zalma? Like the planet Zalma?" Jones didn't answer. "Wow. OK, I'll be quick. Please introduce yourself."

"General Frank Jones. I'm the senior officer in charge of the Roswell crash."

"And what did you find?"

"A decoy lifeboat. As I suspected, they were friendly and wanting our help."

"'As you suspected'?" Baker repeated.

"Yes. Why else would they drop an obvious decoy near the nuclear test site?" *Let's see if she can figure this out.*

"The doctor's report said that the bodies were underdeveloped, with no obvious cause of death. It couldn't be a coincidence that the decoy was dropped above the nuclear test site." He waited for a reply.

"So from the underdeveloped bodies, you determined that it was a decoy, and from the nuclear test site you...."

"If they wanted to steal our weapons, my guess is they would have. By leaving a decoy, they wanted us to know that they were here." He smiled. "I've heard you've read Sherlock Holmes...."

Baker blushed. "Do you want me to figure it out?"

He nodded.

"Oh boy…OK. They wanted you to know that they were here, interested in the weapons, but they didn't steal them. They were testing your reactions with the decoy…like how my communicator was testing *my* reactions!" Baker smiled proudly.

Jones smiled back but didn't continue.

"…So, they need weapons, but they didn't take them because they don't know how to use them?"

"I knew you were smart!" he loudly announced.

Baker beamed at him and clapped her hands.

"Yes, the Zalmen are pacifists. This was confirmed when Privates Dow and Rabinowitz came to my office a couple of days later."

"Privates?"

"Yes, they were back then. I promoted them during our first meeting."

"Ah. I see. So you figured out that the aliens were friendly and needed our help because they were pacifists."

"Yes, they are primarily interested in our negotiators, but I don't believe that will work. I told the president that we must ally with them, or their enemies might come here, and we would have nothing to defend ourselves with."

"So, do we have defenses now?"

"We are in the initial stages, but I'm confident we will be more than ready when needed."

Her expression changed. "How are you different from other generals, and how has that helped?"

He smiled. "You have good questions; I'm glad I hired you." He thought for a moment before responding. "Most generals, or for that matter, most people in the army would have shot first and asked questions later. I was having a hard time discouraging those in my immediate command from doing so."

"You see people differently than most. Can you explain that?"

How do I explain this? He was silent for a few seconds. "I guess I see the good in people. It's my experience that the majority of people only see a person's mistakes, and distance themselves from them because of it. While I do see mistakes as well, I see them as a chance to learn. Mistakes are not something to be embarrassed about, as long as you learn from them."

Baker smiled. "Well said. So, how long is it going to take you to get to Zalma?"

"I can't tell you that quite yet, Miss Baker." Jones got to his feet. "Now, I really must get going. I still have one more thing to take care of before I have to catch my flight."

"Wait! Who's going to record your historical trip?" Baker asked.

You're not going into space. "Well…if you are asking if you can come with…."

"No, but…."

Hmm…. Who can help her out? "Our ambassadors will be joining me and my team. I'll ask Miss Warren to be your eyes and ears."

"Thank you!" Baker said, her face beaming.

CHAPTER SEVENTEEN

FAREWELL

"Well, corporals, I guess this is our last time together until I come back. We will have our monthly check-ins, but those will be short and sweet," Jones said.

Cpl. Dow sighed, making a show of his disappointment. "And we will probably be reporting through General Newman."

Jones chuckled. "Oh, I will be calling you two once in a while, too. I enjoy your point of view on things."

"What are we going to do without you, sir?" Rabinowitz asked.

"I'm a good judge of character, and once General Newman feels respected, he will do the right thing. He's the right man for the job."

"Yes," Dow agreed. "I also have a good feeling."

"*I'm* still learning a lot from you about how we can use anything to our advantage," Rabinowitz said.

Jones smiled, putting a hand on each of the corporals' shoulders. "You're both very fast learners."

"You're a very good teacher," Dow countered, smiling back at him.

"Thank you for believing in us. We're going to miss you," Rabinowitz added.

Jones already had four children, but he could never turn down taking on the role of father-figure, and these two young men were the latest bright souls he'd had the privilege of guiding. Every action they took made his heart swell with pride.

It seemed Dow was thinking along the same lines. "You've been like a father to us this last month."

"Has it only been a month?" Rabinowitz asked.

Jones chuckled. "Oh my, you are right, but what a month! You two have grown so much since that first meeting. I'm so proud of you both."

Dow swallowed like there was a lump in his throat. The men were quiet for a minute. "It's going to be different when you're gone."

Jones cleared his throat. "Yes, well, it's not going to be that long. You keep an eye out for Scornson. He's unpredictable, but if he takes the bait, you shouldn't have to worry about him for a few months."

They all laughed. After the laughter faded,

Rabinowitz asked, "What's that saying you have?"

"The bad guys waste their time arguing with each other, fighting for control. We are stronger than them when we work together!" Jones said.

"It will sure be nice to not have to move every week," Dow said.

Jones shook his head. "No, you still have to do that. Scornson might not be around, but his men still are. I have it all mapped out for you and General Newman."

"Thank you, sir. How do you do it all? How did you know what Newman and Scornson were going to do?" Rabinowitz asked.

"No one knows what's going to happen for sure. I believe it's different for everyone, but when I was around your age, I wrote every little detail that looked out of place. Then, when I was alone, I would dream about it."

"Dream, sir?" Rabinowitz asked.

"Oh, sorry, that's what I called it when I was your age. I think meditate would be a better word. I would meditate and try to guess what could have caused those little details. Then, I wrote that down, along with what I felt when I was having those dreams."

"What you *felt*?" Dow asked.

"You know what I mean. I've seen you react ever so slightly when you get tingles, or the calm that seems out of place. Your hunches, your gut instincts."

Dow dropped his head, chuckled, and nodded.

Rabinowitz's face was blank.

"Yes, trust your gut, and it will serve you well." Jones smiled, then stepped back. "Now where was I...? I would review my notes and see which feelings were right. Eventually, I didn't have to write my notes, and I didn't have to be alone; my dreams and instincts would just kick in. I would examine the facts and attempt to picture the events that led up to it and beyond. In most cases, I was correct."

"Thank you, sir. I will try that as well," Dow said. "You know how I dreamed of flying through space with a ray gun. But I know I have work to do here, and you don't need us to drive you in space."

"Still, you know we wish we were going with you," Rabinowitz said.

Jones chuckled. "And remember, you can call me anytime, but don't mention that to General Newman. I want him to rely on you two and learn to work as a team. Then you can remind him that he has a note-book-sized communicator at his disposal."

They laughed.

CHAPTER EIGHTEEN

THE STING

Gen. Newman entered the DC-3 and saluted to Jones, as did Dow. Jones saluted back.

"At ease."

Newman relaxed and took a seat across from Jones.

With a nod from Jones, Dow headed into the cockpit to join the pilot. Once they were all strapped in, the plane lifted into the air.

When they leveled off at cruising altitude, Jones smiled. "Do you believe in aliens now?"

"Still skeptical, sir," Newman replied. "I do have some questions, though. Assuming I'm not going crazy, what was that device Corporal Dow had, and where did it go?"

Jones leaned back; he expected something like that. "The aliens call it a communicator."

"And you trust these aliens?"

"I have a hunch about them."

Newman went rigid. "What do hunches have to do with it?"

"Plenty. Facts will only get you so far in this world. When facts fail, you have to trust your gut instincts. The president trusts mine."

"The president knows about this?"

Jones let out a chuckle. "Do you want to talk to him?" He pulled out his pocket communicator.

"He has one of those too?" Newman asked with raised eyebrows.

"He does."

Newman looked pale. "I don't know what to think anymore. I'm not going to lie. It was really hard not knowing what the plan was. I'm used to being in control, but for the first time, I trusted someone.... You."

"I'm glad to hear that," Jones said. "I see a bright future ahead for you."

"Thank you, sir. I've learned a lot from you over the past week."

"I take it you don't just mean my stellar chess skills."

Newman laughed. "That too, sir, but when General Scornson offered me a promotion, I told myself I'd do whatever it took to get it, but I realized too late that what it took was more than I was willing to do."

"Well said," Jones complimented.

"So, the aliens…. Tell me about them. That…communicator, you said? It's very impressive."

"Yes, the aliens we know are very technologically advanced pacifists."

Newman crinkled his forehead. "*The aliens we know?*"

"Yes. They're being attacked by other aliens, and they need our help to defend themselves. In return, they will help us defend Earth. Are you OK with that?"

"Sounds like a good deal to me, sir."

Jones glanced down at his wristwatch. "We've got lots of time before we arrive. Why don't I tell you their story?"

"Sure. Why not?"

Jones looked around. "It's too bad we are not on the spaceship right now; they had a room where all the walls, ceiling and floor lit up like a movie theater, but I guess I will just have to do my best to describe it."

"Sounds good."

"The Zalmen are a peaceful people, who developed space travel about a thousand years ago. They were farmers and scientists, not explorers, so they sent out space robot things to search for life in the galaxy rather than do it themselves." Jones leaned forward and whispered, "I thought they were just taking the easy way out, but it turns out that they lack adventure and imagination. I mean, wouldn't you want to fly around and see these new planets for yourself?"

"Yes, sir."

"But I'm getting ahead of myself; now, where was I?" Jones laughed to himself. "Oh yes; they set these space robots to move from solar system to solar system, and if a robot found life on a planet, it would orbit it and monitor communications, continuing to scan and transmit its findings back to Zalma."

"So, the planet is Zalma, and the people are the Zalmen," Newman echoed.

"Yes. They did not find many planets with life, and of the ones that did have life, none had developed space travel until Moad. The Moadites developed space travel, and my guess is that they must not have liked being spied on because they sent a fleet of ships to Zalma."

"So, they must have detected the transmissions and traced them."

"My thoughts exactly. Anyway, the Zalmen tried to communicate with the Moadites, but they wouldn't respond. When the Moad ships arrived, they tried to land but could not get past the deflectors the Zalmen built to protect their planet from meteors. So, the Moadites fired their weapons at the planet. Again, they were unsuccessful."

Newman whistled. "Impressive. Can they set up these deflectors here?"

"I think that is being negotiated." Jones frowned. "Come to think of it, I don't remember seeing it in the agreement." He shook his head. "Anyway, two years ago, the Zalmen detected the first nuclear explosion on our planet—"

"The test in New Mexico?"

Jones nodded. "Soon after, they detected two more explosions where many people died."

"Japan?"

"Very good; you're catching on. I knew you were the right man for the job. Anyway, they wanted peace with the Moadites, not to destroy them, so they continued to monitor Earth's communications, learning our languages, culture, and the status of the war. When they heard we signed the Paris Peace Treaties, they sent a ship to make contact with us."

Newman raised both his eyebrows. "The crash in Roswell?"

"You got it. But it took them five months to fly here, and—" Newman cut him off.

"Wait, I thought there were no planets close enough for—"

"Yes, yes," Jones interrupted, "we asked them about that, and apparently, the theory of relativity does not apply when you can modify gravity."

"So, if you could remove all gravitational forces on the spaceship, you could fly faster than the speed of light?"

"Don't ask me. I didn't study science." He moved his hand over his head. "But if you understood that, then you're going to fit right in."

"So, while they were traveling through space, they ran millions of scenarios of what we might be like, and what would happen in each case."

"Like what would happen if they encountered General Scornson, rather than you?"

"Exactly. They built a space lifeboat, put some dummies in it, and dropped it over the nuclear test site, but the wind carried it to Roswell where Privates Dow and Rabinowitz found it."

Newman frowned. "I thought they were both corporals. Did you promote them for making contact?"

"Yes, and I put Dow in charge of recruiting."

Newman made a triangle with his fingers and was quiet a few seconds. "Are you using his race to weed out people who would be opposed to aliens?"

"Yes, I am."

Newman was quiet for a few more minutes. "But how did the aliens know that you, Dow, and Rabinowitz were safe to contact?"

"They have technology that detects when someone is lying, angry, or hostile."

"So, what about this briefcase? Isn't Scornson following us?"

Jones leaned back, turned toward the cockpit, and called out. "Corporal Dow, update please."

Dow came out of the cockpit. "General Scornson took the bait and flew into Canadian airspace, sir."

Newman was stunned. "Canadian airspace? But the transmitter…."

"It's disabled," Jones explained flatly.

Newman hoisted the briefcase onto his lap and tried the latches. It clicked open. Inside, next to the tracking device and explosive mechanism, was Dow's communicator. It had absorbed itself into the case, so neither Newman nor Lawless could see it. As soon as they were on the plane, it went to work. "How?"

"As I understand it, the device is full of nanites, and they disabled it."

Newman's eyes moved rapidly from one side to the other and he started to sweat. "What are nanites? What are you talking about? Why is he in Canada?"

Jones sent him a soft but firm look. "Nanites are tiny robots. Another flying robot duplicated the tracker signal and flew over several Canadian military bases."

"And General Scornson followed it?"

"He is not the brightest. He never thinks about the consequences of his actions, instead relying only on his own brute strength. Judging by his MO, he was never really interested in me. I'd wager he wants to kill the aliens and take their technology. Can you imagine that? Do you think he would have any chance of figuring out the alien equipment?"

Newman shook his head. "I highly doubt it, but he could always find people to do it for him."

"Unlikely, it operates by voice control, and if it doesn't know you it won't respond. Anyway, I think we should hear what's happening with him; our little decoy should've sent him quite far by now." Jones smiled, then turned to Dow. "Corporal Dow, put the radio on speaker please."

Dow pull"He has one of those too?"ed another communicator from his pocket and tapped it. They could all hear the radio exchange.

"This is Lieutenant Colonel Mitchell of the Royal Canadian Air Force. You have violated Canadian airspace and are ordered to turn around immediately."

"This is General Scornson of the U.S. Army Air Force. I outrank you!"

"I'm sorry, sir, but you are in Canadian airspace without prior authorization. You are ordered to return to American airspace."

"How dare you talk to a Four-Star General of the United States Army that way? I demand that you show me some respect!"

"Sir, you have violated Canadian airspace. If you don't turn around now, we will have no choice but to open fire."

"What about the other plane? I'm tailing a very dangerous fugitive!"

"Sir, you are the only foreign plane on radar."

"That's a lie! Jones's plane is right in front of us. You must see it."

"Mitchell to Base. Are there any other foreign aircraft in the area?"

"Negative. There is no other plane on radar."

"General Scornson, you must turn around now, or we will have no choice but to open fire."

"Oh, I see now. You're harboring those green, filthy, low-life aliens, aren't you? Are you working with Jones? You're not going to stop me. I'll find them."

"Sir, this is your last warning."

Jones knew that the Canadians would not harm an ally unless it was absolutely necessary.

"Pilot, full speed ahead! They won't stop me from finding the filthy aliens' hideout."

There was a long pause, which was filled with the popping of gunfire. Nothing led Jones to believe that the plane had been hit. Scornson didn't seem to care. "How dare you shoot at a U.S. Military aircraft!" he growled.

"Sir, you must land immediately, or we will shoot you down."

"Surrender? Never!"

The radio was once again filled with nothing but static and popping gunfire, before Scornson's voice came through again, this time less crazed and more defeated. "Mayday! Mayday! This is General Scornson to any U.S. Military plane in the area. I'm being shot at, and I need assistance."

Jones picked up his communicator, tapped it, and waited until there was a beep. "This is General Jones. General Scornson, by order of the president, you are to leave Canadian airspace at once."

"*Where are you, Jones? You can't hide! I'll find you—Hey...where did the signal go?*"

"General Scornson, you have performed an unauthorized act of aggression against a foreign government. You are ordered to return to U.S. airspace immediately."

"*Go to H....*" Static cut the transmission.

"Lieutenant Colonel Mitchell, this is General Frank Jones. We request that you be gentle with your intruder. He has not been himself lately."

"'*Not been myself*'! *Where do you get off...? Hey, stop shooting at me! I'm going down!*"

"*General Jones, this is Lieutenant Colonel Mitchell. We will do our best not to injure your officer.*"

"I appreciate that. Jones out." He paused to turn off the radio. "That should keep him busy for a while. The president said he won't be in a rush to ask for Scornson's release."

Newman shimmied in his seat. "So, what now? Am I under arrest?"

Does he still think that?

"Buckle up!" the pilot called out from the cockpit. "We're about to land!"

* * *

"Welcome to Area Four."

It was a bumpy landing; the 'airstrip' was dry desert sand. Once they left the plane, Jones led them to his tent with the notebook-sized communicator. He picked up the device, though he didn't sit down behind the desk. "*Connect me to Ambassador Geogram.*"

Geogram appeared, and Newman leaned forward to take a closer look.

Jones turned the screen slightly so Newman could get a better view. "General Newman, meet Ambassador Geogram from the planet Zalma." He casually handed the device over, and Newman gently accepted it like Jones had handed him a ticking time bomb.

"G-greetings," Newman said.

Geogram tipped his chin forward politely. "Nice to meet you, General Newman."

Jones clapped his hands together. "Wonderful. Shall we get you acquainted in person then? *Jones out.*" He led Newman out of the tent.

Newman followed. At one point on the walk, Jones turned to Newman and crinkled his forehead. "How are you doing with all this so far?"

Newman shrugged his shoulders. "How am I supposed to be doing, sir? My understanding of the world has been turned inside out. What am I even doing here? I thought you were going to arrest me for treason. Aren't you mad that I could have led General Scornson to you?"

That sounds about right. Jones chuckled to himself as he turned to Cpl. Dow, who nodded back at him.

They arrived at a second tent. Jones pulled back the curtain and swept his arm out.

"General Newman, this is Ambassador Geogram in the flesh."

"Hello," Newman said. He reached forward to shake the alien's hand.

Jones smiled. *Newman is taking it better than I expected.* "Our mission here is to protect our planet from hostile aliens and from people like Scornson. If you're going to work with us on this, I need to know if you're OK with everything you have heard and seen so far."

"Yes, sir."

"I want to hear you say it." *Better safe than sorry.*

Newman snapped to attention. His back stiffened. "I'm OK with everything so far, sir. A little over-whelmed, to be honest, but they seem…nice."

"Good." Jones then waved to an empty corner of the tent. "General Newman, I would like to introduce you to Captain Agugua."

Agugua walked out of the invisible Spacevan, and Newman took a small step back.

"You still OK, Newman?" Jones asked with a smirk.

"Yes, sir. Just…why am I really here, sir?"

"Isn't it obvious?" Jones asked.

Newman frowned.

Time for yet another shocker. "I'm recruiting you. I'm heading into space to defend their planet, and I need you to run the operation here."

The Spacevan's invisibility turned off.

"So, you're *not* going to arrest me?" Newman asked.

Jones's lips curled into a smile. "What good would that do? Who would run this place when I'm gone?"

"But…But…. After all I did, you still want me to run this operation, sir?"

Time for the final test. Jones stepped closer to Newman until they were nearly touching. "Did you learn your lesson?"

Newman didn't move, then swallowed. "Yes, sir."

"Good," Jones said. He stepped back, then turned and walked toward the spaceship.

"Um…is that it? You're putting me in charge?"

Jones chuckled to himself. He felt guilty leaving Newman without a proper briefing, but if this was going to work, he needed him to rely on Dow and Rabinowitz. "Don't worry, you are not alone. Corporal Dow has been recruiting more help for you, and Corporal Rabinowitz is your new adjutant. So, are you up for it, General?"

Newman stiffened up again and saluted. "Yes, sir! I would be honored, sir!"

Jones's expression turned serious again. "And remember, no one outside of our group can know about this, not even other generals."

"Yes, sir!"

"You will report directly to our current president for as long as he is in office. Dow will confirm if any future president is safe. He will begin recruiting from other countries as soon as he is done recruiting here."

Newman crinkled his forehead. "We even have to vet future presidents about this?" He paused to think about it. "I guess that makes sense. Yes, sir."

"You're now understanding the importance of all this, aren't you?"

"Yes, sir. This invisibility and nanite technology would be dangerous if anyone outside of our group gained access to it, sir!"

"The president and I have agreed to promote you to lieutenant general to help you in this new role, as you'll need access to highly classified documents. Initially, you'll be reporting to the president on my behalf, but if you play your cards right, I see another promotion in your future very soon."

"Thank you, sir."

"Everything you need to know about the Alliance is in that communicator you are carrying. If you have any questions, you can ask Dow and Rabinowitz. Good luck!" Jones boarded the ship with Agugua, then he turned around and the two generals exchanged salutes.

The spaceship door closed.

Jones looked out the front window to see the spaceship rise above the tents. He noticed that the interior lights switched from white with a blue tinge to white with a red tinge.

"Are we invisible now?" Jones asked.

Agugua spoke into his sleeve, and the computer translated. *"Yes. The lights change as a reminder."*

The ship flew through the clouds at an incredible speed, and Jones continued to be amazed by how they didn't feel like they were moving. The Zalmen said that they had their own pocket of gravity, but that never made any sense to him.

As they reached orbit, Jones saw the shoe-box-shaped ship. "Is the Ymit invisible?"

"Yes," came the captain's translated reply, *"but when we are phased to the same frequency, we can see each other."*

"Interesting."

"Your people are on the second floor," Agugua said. *"With the transparent walls and ceiling, it is the perfect place from which to watch our departure."*

Jones nodded and headed to the gymnasium, and found his team leaning against the transparent walls to get a better look at Earth. It made him nervous.

"Ten-Hut!" Lt. McKenzie called, and the military people straightened. Ambassador Wilcox and Miss Warren looked a little uncomfortable, probably wondering how to react.

"At ease," Jones quickly replied. "There are just a few of us military personnel, and we are on a spaceship, with both alien and human civilians. So why don't we dispense with the formalities?"

The team looked a lot more relaxed.

"And please step away from the windows," Jones said.

"With all due respect, sir, it's not glass. The Zalmen insist that we are safe and there is no way for us to break it. They say there are also deflectors they claim will stop a bullet," Mr. Howard said.

"That's great, but let's not test that." Jones motioned for everyone to step toward him.

Miss Warren took out her communicator. "*Record.*"

Jones continued, "This is a day for the history books…although it may never make it into any."

There were a few chuckles.

"Just in case, Miss Warren is working with Miss Baker to record the events as they unfold. We are the first humans in space!" Jones paused to let that sink in.

While the military personnel stood tall with smiles on their faces, the civilians' eyes popped as they drew closer together.

"We will soon be alone in the vast emptiness of space. If anything goes wrong, there will be no rescue. The Zalmen are five months away, and Earth currently has no space vehicles. In addition, we are basically unarmed, with the exception of a few untested weapons attached to the ship. If anyone wants to return to Earth, this is your last chance."

Everyone remained as they were.

"Good." Jones tapped his communicator. "Captain, we are ready."

The ship slowly turned, so that Earth was above them, and they could see the great blue planet one last time as they made a full orbit.

Jones could clearly make out the continents: North America, Africa, Europe, and Asia, then back to North America before the ship turned and flew past the moon. They looked out the back window at the Earth, which became smaller and smaller until it disappeared.

"It is normal to feel a sense of loss and fear when leaving home to travel the world, but this is different; we just left the world behind. You may feel strong now, or you may feel weak, but sooner or later, you will all feel something, and I want you to know that my door is always open to talk." Jones looked at his team, and while the military men's shoulders sagged, the civilians stood taller.

"Now, let's get down to business. Where are we with everything? Sergeant Abbott?"

"Sir! This is an impressive facility. Anything I ask for seems to grow out of the gymnasium floor. Targets, obstacles, you name it."

"Impressive, thank you. Lieutenant McKenzie?"

"The Zalmen may not be willing or able to fight, but I have been teaching Captain Agugua evasive maneuvers."

"Good. Lieutenant Cameron?"

"The Zalmen have over one hundred years of recordings."

"One hundred years?"

Cameron nodded. "Yes. Apparently, the computer records all foreign transmissions and deletes them when it runs out of space or determines that they are irrelevant. It seems like neither was the case."

Jones frowned. "Everyone should remember that we are dealing with the unknown vastness of space. Anyone could be recording our transmissions as well.

"If they don't have the technology to decrypt our transmissions now, they may someday. So, be careful what you transmit, and definitely don't transmit any technology."

Everyone echoed confirmation, so Jones gestured for Cameron to continue.

"The hard part about decrypting the Moad communications is that their language is more like sounds than spoken words. So, Ambassador Wilcox and I had a hard time knowing when we had a clean signal." Cameron put his hand on Wilcox's shoulder.

"Now that we know this, I am sure we can translate the language," Wilcox added.

"Great," Jones said. "Mr. Howard, what about you?"

"As you mentioned, we attached untested weapons to the hull of this ship. We hope to test them on our way out of the solar system. I'm continuing to learn about Zalmen technology and adapting it to ours. Their laser and plasma cutters look like they may be adapted to weapons."

Everyone had blank faces, not having heard these terms before.

"A laser is a hot beam of light, like a magnifying glass in the sun. A plasma cutter is a very hot flame, and it's extremely dangerous."

Everyone nodded.

"Excellent work! Let's get to it then."

CHAPTER NINETEEN

FIRST SIMULATION

Everyone had just finished their first meal in space together. The dishes were being absorbed into the table by the nanites.

Jones approached Agugua. "Do you understand English? I don't hear my words translated."

Agugua's skin turned red, and he pulled a device out of his ear. He once again spoke in the Zalman language, and a second later, Jones heard the translation spoken from Agugua's silver clothing, which contained the same nanites as his communicator. *"No, I learned very little English on my way here. These devices translate everything you say, blocking out the original speech."*

Jones waited for Agugua to put the device back in before he spoke. "May I have one of these devices as well?"

"Yes, just ask the computer."

"*Computer, can I have one of these translator ear-pieces?*" Immediately a small shelf grew out of the wall, and a similar translator earpiece appeared on top. Jones picked it up and put it in his ear as the shelf melted back into the wall. The earpiece was quite comfortable.

"You will find it will fit perfectly," Agugua said. With the device in his ear, Jones heard English as if Agugua was speaking it directly, without the gap in conversation.

Jones nodded. "It does, thank you. Ambassador Geogram mentioned that you ran simulations on your way here to predict our human response. How does that work?"

"We asked the computer to run a variety of simulations. We started with, *What would happen if we tried talking to a human?* It told us that some would talk, most would run, and some would try to harm us. So, we ran several simulations with the modified clones as decoys to test who reacted the best. We tried several variations of clones, then we asked the computer which was the lowest-risk scenario," Agugua said.

"And could I do that with the Moad?"

"Certainly, just say: *Computer, run a simulation;* followed by your parameters."

"So I could ask it to *run a simulation to see what would happen if we scared the Moad ship off, instead of destroying it, either accidentally or deliberately.*"

Immediately, the walls filled up with text and images.

"What's going on?" Jones asked.

"The computer is running your simulation.... You stated your query after I asked the computer to run your simulation."

"I see...." Jones studied the text, which condensed down to a few lines closest to each of them, in their own languages.

"The computer states that if you scared them off, with no casualties on either side, then the war would frustrate them, and they would just come back in greater numbers," Agugua read from the screen.

"Destroying the ship would lead to a similar result, however; the war would continue longer as the families of those lost would insist on revenge."

"You said if there were no casualties. *What difference would casualties make?*" Jones asked.

Again, the walls were filled with text and images. Then the results were displayed.

"*Minor Moad damage or injuries alone would damage their honor and pride and may result in their desire for revenge or self-destruction. Damage or injuries on our side would give the enemy a false sense of pride and accomplishment, resulting in a shorter war.*"

Jones was shocked. "*Computer, are you saying that in order to win this war, we have to let them win a battle?*"

A voice came from the wall. "*Negative. Only sufficient damage, on both sides, to keep their honor.*"

"*Computer, I believe you are right, but how?*"

"*Insufficient information.*"

Agugua chuckled. "The computer does not come up with the options. You have to find them, and then it can help you pick the best one."

Jones nodded. "Makes sense. By the way, I have been going through your files on the Moadites, and I can't access some of them."

Agugua's skin turned white, and then different shades of blue and green. "I do not know how that would happen. On Zalma, all information is available to everyone. *Communicator, connect us to the council.*"

First Minister Ronderra's image appeared on the wall in front of them. "*Agugua, General Jones, what can we do for you?*"

Agugua bowed his head briefly in respect. "First Minister Ronderra, the general is having problems accessing some files on the Moadites."

The First Minister turned as white as his clothing. "*You should not even see those files; they were believed to be deleted.*"

Agugua turned white. "All information is public. Why is this not?"

"*Everyone who has ever looked at those files has become violently ill. It was decided that they should be removed from our systems.*"

"With all due respect, Minister, I need to know

everything there is to know about our enemies, and I have a pretty strong stomach," Jones said.

Someone from off the screen whispered to the First Minister, "*The Land?*"

Jones had heard native Americans use the term as if it were a living entity, even a god, and wondered if that was the case here.

"Very well, since the computer malfunctioned and the files are still accessible, I will grant you access, provided you do not share its contents with anyone."

"With all due respect, Minister, I may need to share this information with my team. But, as with all classified information, it will be on a need-to-know basis only."

The first minister looked reluctant. He clenched his jaw, then finally said, *"Very well. You have permission to share the files as needed."*

Jones returned to his room and opened the files. The first image was of one species of animal eating another species —the Moadites were carnivores. Of course a vegetarian species would restrict access to this.

"Computer, are all files containing meat restricted from the Zalmen?"

"Yes."

"So, that's why they didn't know we eat meat."

Jones waited for a response but realized that he didn't call the computer's name.

"*Computer, which of these species is dominant?*"

A picture of a reptilian creature appeared on the screen. Jones thought it looked like an alligator body with a turtle's head.

"Hmm. *How many probes have been sent to Moad?*"

"*Only one probe has been sent to Moad. After its capture, the council restricted the planet.*"

"*Captured? By the Moadites? How?*"

"*An unmanned rocket was recorded approaching the probe before it stopped transmitting.*"

"*Did the Moadites reverse engineer the probe?*"

"*Based on the Moadites ship designs, it is probable.*"

"*What technology did the probe have?*"

"*Sub-light speed nuclear drive, navigation computer, transmitter, video camera.*"

"*No deflectors?*"

"*No.*"

"*Good. Were there any other probes lost?*"

"*No other probes were lost. The probes were updated to prevent capture.*"

CHAPTER TWENTY

MORNING EXERCISE

Jones believed that keeping physically fit was good for morale, and both were important on an interplanetary journey. He required and attended morning exercises with the rest of his team and the ship's crew. He usually walked laps with Wilcox, the captain, and the ladies, while his men did the more strenuous exercises.

After the cooldown period, they held an informal meeting to review their progress. Jones sat on a hover chair as he stretched out his legs.

"Sergeant Abbott, anything to report?"

"It's the same old, same old, shooting the same damned stationary targets. Gimme a challenge."

Jones looked around the room. "Is there anyone here who can challenge Abbott?"

After a silence, Howard raised his hand. "These walls and ceilings are made of nanites, right? Could they display moving images for him to shoot at?"

"Yes, I can program that," Joanua said.

"Excellent." Jones nodded. He looked around the room. "What about you, McKenzie?"

"The Zalmen are doing well with basic maneuvers. I'm studying the Moad movements to see if they have any pattern, but so far they have not had any opposition. It's pretty routine. Enter orbit, drop bombs, then leave orbit."

McKenzie stood, looking at nothing, presumably remembering something. "Some interesting things about their ships. They're long, with a transparent cone on the front, presumably a shield to protect the ship. Then something like a Ferris wheel, to generate artificial gravity."

McKenzie smiled and bounced a little. "The wheel's *baskets* are attached to the outside of the wheel when the ship is orbiting, but they turn parallel when the ship is moving. So, the acceleration pushes them to the back of the ship, and to the front of the ship when they are braking."

"Hmm. Impressive design," Howard said.

"Indeed." Jones agreed. "Cameron?"

"Ambassador Wilcox and I have decrypted the Moad transmissions, and we have translated about half of their language and programmed it into the ship's translator."

"Great. Anything to add, Ambassador?"

"I am thinking that we might be able to convince the Moadites to join a trade agreement."

"Interesting. What would you trade for what?"

"Well, you said that the Moadites might try to steal the deflector technology. What if we offer them a trade?"

"It might work," Jones said, "but we would have to ensure that it's only strong enough to protect them from space rocks. I don't want to give them an advantage in a war with us, or any other civilization."

Wilcox looked at Joanua. "Would you be able to find, or design, a low-level deflector like that?"

"Sure, I can do that."

"I would suggest using really old technology. I could also design a self-destruct, so they don't reverse engineer it," Howard offered.

"I could also design a kill switch in case they break the treaty or try to use it against us," Cameron said.

"Good ideas! Well done," Jones praised. "Anything else?"

"I'm also studying the Zalmen culture while teaching Edugra ours. We are making notes that I hope will help our two cultures avoid a faux pas."

"Anything we should know now?"

Wilcox lifted his hand, but then dropped it. "Yes, don't make an OK gesture with your hands."

"Noted." Jones turned his attention to the next man. "Mr. Howard?"

"The weapons attached to the hull of the ship did not test well. Without an atmosphere, most of our weapons have very little effect."

"But if it hits a ship with an atmosphere?" McKenzie asked.

"Yes. If our weapons hit a ship with an atmosphere, it will do damage," Howard replied.

"What about a grenade effect?" Jones asked.

"Yes, we could put an explosive device in a shell with compressed air, and it will have a grenade effect," Howard replied.

"Grenade?" Agugua asked.

"Little pieces of the shell flying everywhere, doing lots of damage," Howard replied.

Agugua nodded.

"I've adapted their laser tool into a ship-size weapon. We don't have anything to shoot out here, so Joanua ran computer simulations. They show it to be an effective weapon, and it's growing on the ship as we speak," Howard said.

"Good work," Jones said.

"I'm working on converting their plasma cutters to weapons. It's the one thing that can cut through Zalma's technology. It's likely a short-range weapon at best," Howard added.

"Good work." Jones thought for a moment. "Could you make a plasma gun or knife? And what about a flaming arrow, crossbow, or catapult?"

"The plasma cutter is already gun-shaped, but it wouldn't be able to shoot," Howard said. "I could make a knife and some kind of projectile. But again, you have to be careful with these devices, as we are on a ship in the middle of space. If they puncture the wall…."

The room was silent. They all knew the consequences.

"Thank you." Jones got to his feet. "Captain Agugua was showing me the computer simulations. We have just been through war, and I don't think any of us want to go through that again."

Abbott grunted.

Jones smirked. "Except for Abbott, of course. Anyway, with Zalma technology, we have the upper hand with the Moad. However, I am concerned that if we let them know our capabilities, they will try to negotiate or steal it."

Jones waited as his words sank in and people nodded their heads. "The computer simulation suggested that if we put up a strong front and scare them off, they will be humiliated, lose their honor, and want revenge. So, I would like to allow minor damage to allow them to keep their honor, while not losing life on either side. Suggestions?"

Abbott grunted. "If we aren't going to fight, why did you bring me?"

Jones chuckled. "I didn't say that we wouldn't fight. I said that we shouldn't kill. There is a difference."

"So, injuries and torture are OK?" Abbott asked.

"Injuries, yes. Torture, no. We don't want them to feel the need for revenge. Come to think of it, you are the best person for this job."

Abbott was silent and looked at Jones, dumbfounded.

"I want you to think of fighting us. What could we do to convince you not to fight with us?"

"Hmm... I don't know. This feels like an insult. I live to fight, not to avoid a fight. Why did I sign up for this mission? When I was asked if I liked aliens, I thought I was going to get a chance to fight them. Then I found out that I might, but I had to fly through space for five months with some chromedome pacifist vegetarians first."

Jones frowned. "Watch it, Sergeant."

Abbott looked down. "I'm sorry, sir. It's just that everyone here is so nice and fragile, it makes me sick. There's no one here who can challenge me, and I'm going stir-crazy trying to keep myself busy."

"Yes, we talked about this just a few minutes ago," Jones said.

Abbott shook his head. "...And now you're telling me that when we get there, I can't fight! You're killing me, General. Is it too late to turn around, or can I take that Spacevan thingy back to Earth?"

Agugua grunted. "The *thingy* is not designed for interstellar travel. It would most likely take you one of your years to fly back, and it cannot hold that much food."

Abbott paced back and forth, grumbling. "So, what am I going to do? I've got to do something, or you might as well kill me now."

"Would you like to learn to fly?" McKenzie asked. "I can teach you. It might not be hand-to-hand combat, but it'll give you something to do, and something to shoot at."

Abbott thought for a moment. "Hmm…. I don't know. I suppose it's better than nothing. I'll try it."

Jones hummed. "That's good for now. I would like everyone to come up with at least one idea on how to give the enemy honor, without losing a life on either side. Dismissed."

Jones decided to call Earth only once a month for a report. On the one-month anniversary of their leaving Earth, Jones video called General Newman on the communicator. "How are things going back on the homestead?"

Newman smiled. *"Dow's doing well. His instincts are incredible. Few failed recruits, and he is now recruiting outside of the army as well."*

"Good."

"Yes, and he's found the most amazing university graduate, someone who can actually understand the Zalmen technology."

Jones raised his eyebrows. "What's his name?"

Newman grinned. *"Her name is Dr. Mary Goss. It's interesting, the male engineers seem to accept the aliens with no problem, but they won't accept the ladies."*

Jones raised his eyebrows. "Hmm... That's not good. What are you doing about it?"

Newman assumed his thinking posture, forming a triangle with his fingers. He seemed to ponder the question for a long time before he spoke. *"Well, Mr. Harper is the senior on the project, but he refuses to attend Sarara's classes, or work with Dr. Goss."*

Jones grunted. "If I may give some advice?"

Newman nodded. Jones didn't miss the eager glint in his eyes; Newman was still looking to please, but in a different way. I think he wants me to see that he's willing to learn. *Well that's progress.*

"They're civilians, not soldiers. You might be doing this already, but give them space to work out their problems. If they don't, then remind them who the general is."

Newman smiled. *"Thank you, sir. I've learned a lot from your example and am giving them the chance to learn from their own mistakes."*

Jones smiled. "Good. By the way, it looks like the Moadites had captured and reverse-engineered the probe sent to their planet. Luckily, it was old technology, but we should match it. They tell me Kanara should be able to give you the probe's design."

"Match it? You don't want to put up a strong front?"

Jones shook his head. "Just like on Earth, if they knew our capabilities, they would be afraid of it or try to copy or steal it. And with good reason, with our joint technology, we could easily destroy them."

Newman tilted his head. *"I don't follow. Isn't that what we do?"*

Jones grunted. "Imagine if we could time travel back to the Alamo with a sniper rifle or machine gun, and win the battle."

Newman smiled. *"That would be good."*

"But now imagine that instead of winning, the enemy stole the gun or rifle and reverse engineered it."

"That could be devastating, not just for us, but other countries as well."

"Exactly! The Zalmen and I would like to resolve this peacefully, and without letting them know our full capabilities. They know Zalma has deflectors and the sub-light drive on the probe. Other than that, I don't want them to know we have anything more than they do. If they have nuclear bombs, we can use nuclear bombs, but remember, the Zalmen don't want us to hurt their enemy. Scare them, yes, hurt them, no."

"Sounds like you have your work cut out for you."

Jones nodded. "Yes I do, and I imagine you do too."

"So what's your plan?"

"I don't know yet. I'll let you know next time." Jones sighed as he disconnected the video call. If only coming up with a plan was as easy as asking that question.

CHAPTER TWENTY-ONE

UNIFORMS

After morning exercise, while everyone was cooling down, Jones asked, "Has anyone come up with what we can do to give honor without death?"

Lt. McKenzie stepped forward to speak. "If we engage them with small remote-controlled fighter planes, there would be some lag time, and those ships are more likely to be destroyed with no loss of life."

"Great job!" Jones smiled. "What else have you been working on?"

"Mr. Howard and I have been working on the battle simulations with Abbott and the bridge crew. We have expanded it to multiple ships on both sides. Captain Agugua is learning defensive moves, and our general here has participated in commanding the fleet."

Jones nodded. "Yes. I'm used to battling on the ground. It's a challenge to think vertically." He turned to Cameron. "Lieutenant?"

"I'm sorry I didn't come up with any honor-without-death ideas, but I like McKenzie's fighter plane suggestion! Wilcox and I have decrypted the Moad transmissions. We have determined that their goal is to steal Zalma's technology and take the Zalmen as slaves."

"Anything to add, Ambassador?"

"Yes. Joanua and the men have built a low-level deflector, with a self-destruct and kill switch. With your permission, we would like to do the same with artificial gravity modules."

"Very good. Anything else?"

"I have written up a peace proposal and trade agreement for the Zalma council to review."

"And what are you proposing that they trade in exchange?" Jones asked.

"As with us, I doubt there is much that the Moadites will have to offer the Zalmen. However, they might have stories or they might have things that *we* could trade the Zalmen for stories."

"Good job." Jones turned. "Mr. Howard?"

"The computer simulations show that the laser cutters should cut through the Moad hull enough to cause air leaks."

"Can we use it to disarm them in some way?"

"I don't know. Like submarines and bombers, their weapons are internal. Maybe we could weld the bomb bay doors shut?"

"That would be good." Jones turned to Abbott. "Sergeant?"

"The flight training is going well. I can almost take off and land without crashing. But, as for this place, I am getting bored with the moving targets. Sure, they are better, but I can only shoot at targets so many times, and the only one of you with field training is McKenzie, and he's not that much of a challenge. I'm worried I'm going to break his bones or accidentally kill him." Abbott shook his head.

Jones cleared his throat.

"Oh, I am sorry, General. I know you have combat experience too, but I am not risking injuring or killing you."

Agugua stood, his normally blue skin was now bright yellow showing his anger. "I have had enough of your whining! You insult us every chance you get. You call us 'chromedomes' and you eat meat with your bare hands. You are barbaric and an insult to humans!"

Everyone in the room was shocked. No one moved as Agugua marched forward, putting himself nose to nose with a red-faced Abbott. The sergeant was vibrating with barely restrained fury.

That was what spurred Jones to action. He stepped forward, prepared to get between them to calm things down, but Agugua held up his hand. Jones stopped and watched in silence. Tension continued to build between the captain and the marine.

Suddenly, a malicious grin formed on Abbott's face, and his muscles tensed as he reared his fist back an inch, then delivered a sucker punch straight to Agugua's gut. *No! Stop! This is* not *the way,* Jones thought, but Agugua didn't even move. It was as if the punch hadn't even affected him.

A second later, Abbott grunted. His eyes were wide with disbelief, surprise, and...pain? Jones kept watching. *What is happening? What is Agugua planning?* he wondered, still not moving from his place.

Abbott slowly withdrew his fist. He maintained eye contact with Agugua, though Jones could see that he was trying to hide the pain he was in. Agugua just smiled back as his skin color returned to blue. He seemed happy with the result—almost smug. He had things under control.

For now, at least. *Did Zalmen have a unique physiology that Agugua could withstand such a hit and cause Abbott pain? Is Zalmen skin more like leather?*

The silence broke. With a satisfied growl, Abbott stepped back and flexed his muscles, then took up a boxing position. His right hand struck first, then his left, aiming for the ribs and jaw. Abbott delivered a series of rapid punches to the captain's gut, up the torso, and finally pulled his right arm back behind his shoulders while the left went beside the captain's head. He was preparing for a devastating blow directly to the face.

Jones moved again; this was getting out of hand.

Before Jones even got close enough to make a difference in the fight, Abbott's whole body twisted and he let out a yell. Instead of hitting the captain's face, Abbott's arm went over Agugua's head. A frustrated yell left his lips, and then Abbott's leg wrapped around the back of Agugua's as Abbott tried to use his momentum to pull the captain over.

The captain remained unmoved. His face was calm. Jones stopped again, puzzled. *How? What is going on?*

Abbott increased his speed and he performed several other rapid-succession moves, fists and knees flying but continuously diverted.

Jones's eyes popped. *What is* happening? Worry shot through him as Abbott withdrew his knife.

Without hesitation, Abbott stabbed the knife downward, aiming for Agugua's leg. Again, at the last second the blade was diverted. Was he missing intentionally? Jones didn't even realize it was possible to feint so many moves in a row. He was confused but impressed.

Then Abbott dropped his knife and grabbed his service revolver, aiming it at the captain's shoulder—

"Enough!" Jones leaped forward to grab Abbott's gun. Too late—

He just shot the captain!

Time stood still as Jones thought of the ramifications of Abbott's actions. *How am I going to explain this to the Zalma council?*

Jones grabbed Abbott's gun and turned it on him. "What did you do? Shooting an ally? You're confined to quarters until further notice!"

"There is no need for that."

Jones turned to Agugua and saw the bullet, frozen in place, barely touching Agugua's clothing before it fell to the ground.

Everyone was silent until....

Agugua laughed out loud. "That was...satisfying? I do not remember experiencing such an...adrenalin rush? Is that what you call it?"

All the humans were in shock as their mouths hung open.

"You're alright?" Jones asked.

"Yes. I feel much better after...venting? Is that what you call it?" Agugua replied.

There was silence again.

Joanua chuckled, and the humans looked at her. "What, don't your clothes protect you?"

"Protect us how?" Jones looked back and forth between Agugua and Joanua. "Are you saying that this was a demonstration?"

"A demonstration, yes," Agugua replied.

"The clothing protects us in a variety of ways. The

material can harden and, in some cases, generate small deflector fields, as you saw with the bullet," Joanua replied.

The humans looked at each other, not knowing what to say.

Agugua chuckled. "Did you not wonder why we were never afraid of you humans? No offense, but you are a violent species. If you tried to inflict injuries on us, we have no skills to defend ourselves."

Jones looked over at the captain. "Are you saying that your clothing protected you against Abbott?"

"Yes," Agugua replied.

"YYEESSsss!!!" Abbott yelled as he stretched his arms out wide and hugged the captain.

Jones was not impressed by the sergeant's actions, but when Agugua returned the hug and they both laughed, Jones relaxed and returned Abbott's revolver to him. "Demonstration or not, you're still confined to quarters for one week, except for meetings and scheduled exercises."

Abbott grunted, but did not object.

"We can make you clothing like this as well," said Joanua.

Jones raised an eyebrow. He eyed the shapeless silver foil suit she was wearing. "Can you make it look more like our uniforms?"

"I can, but we would have to make it thicker." She picked up her tablet and tapped it. A sample picture was displayed on the wall. It looked the same, but bulkier, like a doll wearing denim.

Jones grunted.

"Sir, if I may...." Miss Warren raised her hand. "I can work with Joanua and Sergeant Abbott to smooth out the edges and test its functionality."

"Thank you, Miss Warren."

The next day, Donna came in, wearing a sky-blue blouse and a black skirt. Abbott whistled. She smiled as she handed a golden-brown uniform to Jones. Joanua handed more blue clothing out to the rest of the humans, then they stood back.

Jones held out his clothing, a golden-brown suit jacket with a gold dress shirt and tie, then looked at the others, who were doing the same. "These are different."

"Yes, I thought your new department, including all of us, should have our own special uniforms. We're a team, and I thought we should look like one. I hope I didn't overstep."

"Hmm. I don't normally like civilians dressing in military uniforms, but this is a unique situation, being in space and all, and we are all part of this great adventure. Permission to wear space uniforms granted."

Donna smiled. "There are subtle variations. The civilians have less formal versions with polo shirts. I picked blue because the sky is blue, and we are in the sky. Black pants, because space is black. When I thought about material, the only thing close to that thickness is a twill weave like fatigues and denim."

"This doesn't look or feel like either."

Donna chuckled. "No, I didn't think you would approve of wearing denim jeans, but I thought you would approve of silk with a twill weave."

"Silk isn't this elastic."

Donna turned red. "Oh, you noticed. I had to use another material with the silk to make it more flexible."

"Well, what did you use?"

"Nnnnylon?" she said sheepishly.

"Like the material in your stockings?"

Donna, still red-faced, nodded.

Jones pulled the material. It was smooth and strong, plus it was very flexible. "Well, it looks like it should do the trick. And this material has the same protection as their silver clothing?"

"It does," Joanua confirmed. "The material is made up of nanites that change the material as needed. So, if someone tries to hit you, it can change to steel, or into a deflector."

Jones's forehead wrinkled. "It actually changes the material and makes things?"

"Yes, just like your communicator does. To avoid detection, it is just a normal piece of metal, but when you want to talk, it creates the circuitry to do so."

"Interesting. That's why our scientists couldn't find anything. Then, does the clothing also work as a communicator?"

Joanua nodded.

"What about functionality? Did it stand up to Sergeant Abbott's test?"

"Um…." Donna's face went red again. "He wouldn't try the clothing on. He said he didn't need it, so we ran computer simulations based on his movements with Captain Agugua."

Abbott's face turned red hot. "You recorded that!"

Joanua raised her forehead. "You attacked our captain. Did you think that our ship would not record you?" Abbott's anger died. "What angle do you want it from?" She tapped her communicator a few times and the walls, ceiling, and floor lit up with dozens of videos of him from the appropriate angles. While some of them were him in his current uniform, some showed him in the new uniform he refused to wear, others showed his skeleton, and others showed his muscles.

Abbott rolled his eyes. Joanua chuckled and stopped the videos.

Donna stared at Abbott; she seemed amused by his disgruntled expression, but also like she wanted to comfort him with a hug. When she noticed that Jones was looking at her, she continued, "And as Joanua mentioned, the material works like the communicator, so if you don't like the color, you can change it with a voice command, or the push of a button."

Again, Joanua tapped her communicator a few times, and all the Zalma uniforms changed to blue and black to match Donna's uniforms.

Jones nodded his approval. "Now, we all are a team. We just need a name.... We already have Army Air Force."

"Space Force?" Abbott suggested.

Jones considered it for a moment. "Sounds tacky."

"Star Force?" Mr. Howard said.

"Better."

"Star Allies...Planetary Peacekeepers...Alliance of Planet Peacekeepers...The Galaxy's Peacekeepers?" Ambassador Wilcox suggested.

"Those sound better. Let's see if we come up with any more, and vote on it tomorrow," Jones said.

CHAPTER TWENTY-TWO

BLUE-SPECKLED ROCK

Jones looked around. The terrain was unfamiliar to him. "Blue-speckled rock?"

"Probably has copper crystals," Howard replied.

The crevice they took refuge in provided good protection, but they couldn't stay there long. Jones motioned for Cameron to go left, and Jones went right, leaving the civilians in the middle. Before he rounded the corner, he motioned Howard to look.

Howard lifted his head slightly to peek over the rock, but a bullet ricocheted off the rock before they heard the shot. Jones was glad they were wearing the protective uniforms. The flash from the rifle came from some red bamboo like vegetation, giving him what he needed. He heard another shot, probably from Cameron. Knowing the enemy's position, Jones continued around the bend to get a better shot.

The green clothing was clearly visible through the vegetation. He slowly aimed his rifle and fired. But out of the corner of his eye he saw something covered in the red vegetation lunge out at him.

Jones grabbed his knife and swung it at the beast, but he missed. The beast landed on top of him, and the two of them went rolling. Jones swung again, but the beast blocked his move and threw Jones to the ground. Rolling into a kneeling position, Jones got his first good look at the enemy. It was a man, but he must have made the red vegetation into some kind of paint and covered himself with it. A few branches stuck out of what little clothing he was wearing.

The man pulled out a device from his belt, and a blue flame glowed from it. It was most likely a plasma weapon, the only thing that could penetrate the Zalma technology.

As the man leaped forward, there were several gunshots, and the man fell to the ground.

Cameron, Howard, and Wilcox came out of the vegetation.

"Good game," Jones said as he extended his hand toward the body, but the body came to life and bounced into a fighting position.

Abbott took Jones's hand and shook it. "Good game, but how did you beat me?"

Cameron chuckled. "The general knew that you would target him. After I shot at you, he knew you would go in the opposite direction, where you would expect him to be. But he also knew you would no longer be watching for us, so we were free to sneak up on you."

Jones nodded. "It's not just a game of strength; it's also a game of strategy."

"I forgot you were the best. I'll be more careful next time," Abbott said.

"You were going to use a plasma dagger on me?" Jones asked, disappointment clear in his tone. "You know that they can cut through Zalma's technology, including these uniforms."

Abbott's face flushed bright red. "No.... Yes.... Well, sort of. It has safeties in it, and the flame turns off before it does any real damage."

Abbott turned the dagger on and pushed the flame into his other hand. You could see that it hurt, but as the dagger got closer, the flame went down until it touched his hand and the flame was gone. "They tell me that it won't do that if I am battling a real enemy."

Abbott sighed. "But these bullets really sting. What did you put in them?"

"They are made of nanites," Howard said.

"Of course...." Abbott replied.

"It's a normal bullet until you fire them, then they can change into whatever seems appropriate. For the purpose of these games, I believe it became hard rubber."

"How did it go?" Joanua asked as she walked through the vegetation.

"It was great!" Cameron replied.

Jones turned to Joanua. "How do we clean up?"

"Are you finished?" she asked.

"Yes."

"*Computer, reset gymnasium,*" she said.

Immediately, the vegetation began to shrink, and the floor returned to varnished hardwood. Joanua took the vegetation off of Abbott and put it on the injuries on his back. The vegetation turned into a gel, and then a bandage.

Abbott struggled to remove it. "Thanks, but I want to feel the pain. It's good motivation."

Abbott put the bandage on his hand instead. Joanua looked confused.

"Self-inflicted," Abbott said.

Joanua still looked confused.

"What planet was that?" Wilcox asked.

"It was mostly Zalma but had a few Earth elements," Joanua replied.

Jones couldn't believe his eyes. "How does all this work?"

"It was Lieutenant Cameron's idea." Joanua turned a little more purplish when she said his name.

Jones was about to congratulate Cameron, but stopped himself. The lieutenant was blushing brightly at the praise. It made Jones smirk, because Cameron was usually indifferent to praise. *But not from pretty ladies.* Jones glanced to the side and saw that Wilcox was also watching Cameron; it seemed he wasn't the only one who noticed.

"Yes," Cameron stuttered. "I thought that if the nanites could reconfigure to make targets and communicators, why not a training field?"

"Everything you see is nanites that reconfigure themselves to be the plants, rocks, or whatever," Joanua replied.

Jones opened his eyes wide. "But where did it get all those nanites? They couldn't all be in the floor."

"No, most of it was hollow, about the thickness of an eggshell, but thicker when you were close, to give a real feel to them," Joanua replied.

"Can you eat the plants?" Wilcox asked.

Joanua chuckled. "You can, but I wouldn't recommend it. The nanites create an accurate replica of the plant. It would taste the same, but it would convert back to nanites in your stomach and flush out the usual way."

"Like plaster props that actors use," Donna guessed from where she leaned in the gymnasium's doorway. "You wouldn't want to eat fake fruit either, no matter how real it looks." She smiled around at them all, though her eyes trailed a second longer over Abbott.

"Precisely," Joanua agreed.

* * *

Jones called General Newman on the communicator. "How are things going back on the homestead?"

Newman smiled. *"Mr. Harper and Dr. Goss are still not working together. Harper has been building a space version of the X1 he designed to break the sound barrier. Dr. Goss has some great ideas but can't build them. They're progressing well, but if they would work together, we would be way ahead of the game."*

Jones hummed.

"How's the flight?"

Jones sat back. "Well, since I talked to you last. Abbott was starting to get restless and bored. He needed a physical challenge, and none of us are strong enough. So the Zalmen gave us their suits with deflectors that can stop a punch or even a bullet. Apparently, they have been wearing them this whole time."

"This whole time?"

"Yes. Ms. Warren designed new uniforms for us. We are sending the pattern and fabric to your Spacevan. If the president approves, your team can wear them as well."

"Interesting. I will follow up on that."

"We have our uniforms only blocking us from getting seriously hurt, and it cushions the blow when we fall. We are now running war game simulations twice a week."

Newman chuckled. *"Sounds like fun."*

Jones chuckled. "It is. I thought my days in the field were over. However, with this protective clothing, we give Abbott a good challenge."

Newman raised his eyebrows. *"Really? I can't wait to see this protective clothing."*

"Ambassador Wilcox has reviewed a lot of the Zalma history; he tells me it's boring. No wars, very little conflict."

"Sounds like heaven."

"Doesn't it?"

Wilcox entered Jones's quarters. "Sir, can we talk?"

"What's on your mind, Ambassador?"

"In many states, interracial couples are still illegal. What's your opinion?"

Jones grinned and closed the door. "I think you and Edugra make a great couple."

Wilcox raised his eyebrows. "Edugra?"

Jones chuckled. "You are an ambassador, and isn't there a thing called diplomatic marriages?"

Wilcox grimaced. "That's usually for kings, and other rulers, and of the same species. How did you know it was *her*?"

Jones sat back. "The amount of time you two spend together."

"I just noticed Cameron's awkward movement around Joanua, and it made me wonder," Wilcox said.

Jones nodded. "I noticed it myself. I don't think they know either."

Wilcox chuckled. "Anyway, we spend so much time together because it's my job to learn their culture, but how do I know it's love?"

Jones put on his best poker face. "If you are asking, that probably means that it is. When you think of her, who's needs are you thinking about?"

Wilcox turned red. "What do you mean?"

"Are you thinking about your needs, and what she can do for you?"

"No, of course not. I want to make her happy, do what's best for her."

"So, you are trying to impress her, make her fall in love with you?"

"No, it's not like that. Oh, I can't explain it, never mind." He stood to leave.

Jones held up his hand and gestured to sit. "Sorry, I was testing you. What you're saying does sound like love." He paused. "Did you know my wife is from France?"

Wilcox looked Jones in the eye.

"Yes, it might not be the same, but there were cultural barriers on both sides that we still have to deal with."

"I suppose so, but…."

Jones held up his hand. "Cross culture is still cross culture. Sure, you might have the extra hassle of having external groups hating you, but dealing with a lady and her family is still the same."

"Are you serious? Edugra is from another planet! I am sure most people envy you when they see you together. Very few on either side will accept us."

Jones cocked his head. "It's true that American men adore French women, but her French parents were not so fond of losing their daughter, nor was she wanting to leave her country."

"I supposed that may be the same," Wilcox said, then paused. "Thank you for your time, sir." He shook hands and left.

CHAPTER TWENTY-THREE

X20

Jones video called General Newman on the communicator.

Newman cringed. *"Our first space flight was…."*

Jones raised an eyebrow. "Doesn't sound good…."

"Mr. Harper built and launched his X20, and with his pilot, successfully reached the moon."

"But…."

"They launched a nuclear torpedo and detonated it at five miles. Apparently, this generates an electromagnetic pulse, that overloaded all the electrical systems on the ship, and the blast caused micro-fractures in the ship's hull."

"Not good. So, what happened?"

"Dr. Goss, Mr. Quinn, and the Zalmen created what they call a gravity gun to rescue them."

"Did it work?"

"Yes, the two men are safe. Then Mr. Harper stepped

down from being lead engineer, and Mr. Quinn took over. Dr. Goss is now in charge of the department."

Jones smiled. "Good progress."

"Yes. Dr. Goss realized that the Zalma technology is too advanced for the men, and restructured the learning process. She now learns from Sarara, teaches Quinn, and he teaches the other men, with Goss's help."

"Great progress. Well done."

"How's the flight?"

Jones sat back. "Well, since I talked to you last, Sergeant Abbott has managed to teach the Zalmen self-defense moves."

Newman raised his eyebrows. "Really? That's great!"

Jones sighed. "Yes, but it feels like we are selling apples in the garden of Eden."

Newman sat back. "Oh, I understand."

"Ambassador Wilcox is now writing a peace proposal for the Moadites, but I doubt they will listen."

Newman nodded.

"Lieutenant McKenzie and Mr. Howard have continued their battle simulations with the bridge crew. Captain Agugua is now comfortable taking the lead diplomatically, then turning it over to McKenzie for battle."

"That's good. And what about Moad?"

"We know that we have the upper hand. I have reviewed several videos of their previous attacks, and it looks like the ships attacking have evolved over the decades. Since they haven't had any resistance, it looks like most of the space ships are bomber style, with no defenses. The early ships looked different and may have had ship to ship weaponry, but we don't know as there was no reason for them to use it. We know they can't get past our deflectors, so we have the luxury of taking it slow."

"Yes."

"In the computer simulations, it seems that the best possible outcome is to give the Moad honor and pride by sacrificing a few unmanned fighters."

"Sacrifice our ships, sir?"

"Yes. We are dealing with a different scenario here, aren't we? We have the upper hand with this technology, but we don't want another Hiroshima, do we? Death on either side will just escalate things, create vendettas and prolong the war. Intimidating them could be just as dangerous."

Newman leaned back in his chair and formed a triangle with his hands. *"I see."*

"If we acknowledge their needs, while showing superiority, they will realize that this is a war they are not going to win."

"Yes, that could work. How about the gravity gun?"

"You mentioned that earlier. What does it do, and how does it work?"

"It changes the gravity on an object. For the rescue, Dr. Goss said something about increasing the gravity of the

metal, or magnetizing the hull, as she called it. It can also pull an object closer, or push it away. So, the same device was used to tow the disabled ship back to Earth."

"Impressive. I wish you could send the plans for it to our people to take a look at, but even with these highly encrypted communications, I just don't want to take the chance transmitting technology."

"I agree. Better safe than sorry, sir."

"Well, I'll mention the idea to my team and see if they can come up with anything. I'll let you know next time." He disconnected the call, then pressed the ship intercom button. "All available personnel to the briefing room in five minutes."

Jones addressed his team and the ship's crew. "Our new scientist back on Earth, Dr. Mary Goss, has theorized something she calls a gravity gun. I wish she could transmit her work to us, but I don't want to take the risk of transmitting technology. Any idea what it could be, and could we design and build it here?"

"Sounds interesting. What's it in reference to?" Mr Howard asked.

"Oh, I guess I should tell you that the Earth team has successfully launched a ship to the moon!"

The humans cheered.

"But it quickly went south when they launched a nuclear torpedo and an electromagnetic pulse fried the ship's electrical systems."

"Of course it did," Joanua said matter-of-factly.

The humans all turned to her.

"A nuclear detonation generates an electrical pulse. Everyone knows that."

Jones cleared his throat. "Anyway, Dr. Goss and her team used this gravity gun to increase the gravity of the metal, or magnetize the hull, which sealed the fractures and then they used it to tow the disabled ship back to Earth."

Joanua's skin turned green. "It sounds like she reversed a deflector."

Mr. Howard raised his eyebrows. "What do you mean reverse?"

Joanua blinked. "Our deflectors use negative gravity to push objects away. We could use positive gravity to pull."

Jones and his team shouted at almost the same time. "You can change gravity?"

Joanua's skin flashed white in alarm, and she shrunk back in her chair. "Yes. It is one of our basic skills."

Mr. Howard reached across the table and held her hand and smiled. "It's okay; they are not angry with you; they are just surprised."

Joanua's color returned to normal fern as she slowly sat back up. "Oh, okay."

Wilcox turned to the rest of the team. "Yes, Geogram told me this as well. He said they would share the knowledge with us, and I guess they did on Earth, it just never came up in conversation here until now."

Mr. Howard chuckled. "I guess it didn't." He turned to Joanua, "Can you teach me now?"

"Oh, of course I can, it's easy."

The humans laughed.

CHAPTER TWENTY-FOUR

ATTACKED

.

"Everyone to the conference room." It was Edugra's voice, but she had never used the ship-wide intercom like that before, and her voice was stressed.

When Jones entered the conference room, he saw what he assumed was a live video feed from Zalma.

Captain Agugua stood beside the screen. "The deflectors are failing again. We all knew it would happen, but we thought we would get there in time. We are still two months away."

"How long do they have?" Jones asked.

"The Zalma scientists calculate a seventy-three percent chance that they will survive this round, but only an eleven percent chance that they will survive the next."

"The next?" Mr. Howard asked.

Agugua turned to Howard. "Moad is six of your light-years from Zalma. It takes the Moadites several years to travel at sub-light speed. But they have several ships constantly rotating between planets. About every twenty-six days, a ship arrives, attacks, firing everything that they have, and then returns home."

"How long are their attacks?" Sergeant Abbott inquired.

"Only a few days," Agugua replied.

"When the alliance was signed, Zalma was under attack, and the deflectors were failing. We talked your scientists through modulating the deflector frequency to be more effective against the Moadites' new weapons. Will that work again?" Jones asked.

"They have tried that as well, and it has not helped," Joanua replied.

"What about the evacuation?" Jones inquired.

"Only about half the population has been evacuated, and the other half is refusing to leave," Agugua said.

Jones sighed. "Are we going as fast as we can?"

"We are, sir."

"Is there anything we can do to move faster? Can we jettison cargo to make the ship lighter?" Lt. McKenzie asked.

Joanua shook her head. "No, our gravity drive doesn't work that way. Our weight doesn't affect our speed." Suddenly, her eyes lit up. "You mentioned last time that Dr. Goss strengthened the hull with a gravity beam. I think you called it *magnetizing the hull*."

Jones nodded.

"I think that we can use that to strengthen our hull and double our speed."

"Great!" Jones looked around at the others. "Any other thoughts on how to help Zalma right now?"

Ambassador Wilcox raised his hand. "I could try to offer the Moadites a gift, a sample of the proposed technology."

"Do we know that they have received and understood our messages?" Jones asked.

"Yes, we sent the messages on their channel un-encrypted. Then, we heard them discussing our offer on their encrypted channel, but their opinion seems to be: Why trade what they can take?"

"Then a gift will not help. Anything else?" Jones looked around.

Howard raised his hand. "Could we send the Zalmen instructions to build weapons?"

Edugra sighed. "And who is going to fire them? Remember, my people are pacifists."

Wilcox leaned forward. "A computer?"

Joanua hummed. "Maybe...."

"This would be all well and good," Jones interrupted, "but secure communications or not, I don't feel comfortable transmitting technology. Someone could intercept it, and no matter how encrypted you make it, it's only a matter of time before someone decodes it."

The room was silent for about a minute.

Joanua's eyes lit up. "Sarara said that her new student theorized using an Einstein–Rosen bridge as a new way to communicate."

Jones nodded. "Dr. Goss. What did she come up with?"

"The theory is that two black holes might create a strong enough gravitational field to connect the two points on a quantum level, so that travel between the two points is instantaneous."

Jones raised an eyebrow. "Are you saying that we could instantly appear on Zalma?"

"Unfortunately not." Joanua sighed. "The connection is so small that only a signal can get through."

Lt. Cameron gulped. "So we need to find a black hole?"

Joanua giggled. "No, we need to create a gravitational field as strong as a black hole."

"That sounds dangerous," Wilcox said, his eyes wide.

Joanua nodded. "Yes, we would have to create a gravitational force stronger than a sun, and contain it so that it doesn't crush us."

"I agree with Ryan. That sounds too dangerous," Donna said. "I don't think it's worth the risk."

"I admit that there is a significant risk, but with our gravity technology, it is possible. To run the tests, I suggest we use probes and launch them a safe distance away."

Captain Agugua turned green. "And what would you call a safe distance?"

Joanua's skin fluttered through multiple shades of green, teal, and purple. "Out of any solar systems. For us, we could run a probe on a parallel course, about a billion miles away."

Jones frowned. "Are we benefiting anything from doing all that? What's the point of this if we have to broadcast over a billion miles?"

Joanua turned red. "Sorry sir, the distance is just for the tests. If we create a black hole, but do not contain it, we could destroy a solar system, but out here, we only have to worry about us."

Jones felt heat rush to his face. "Oh."

Joanua chuckled. "Luckily, it would destroy the probe and disappear, so it should be safe to test as long as nothing is close enough to be sucked in during that short time. Once we know we can contain it, we can move it closer."

"How much closer?" Howard asked.

"That depends on the test results. If the gravitational forces are one hundred percent contained, we could attach it to the ship."

Donna frowned. "That sounds like a lot of dangerous work. Is it worth it?"

"I believe so, if we want totally secure communications."

Jones held his hand up. "So, you're saying that you could send a signal that no one else would be able to intercept?"

"In theory, yes."

"How sure are you that we can do this?"

"Right now, I would say it could go either way. I would have to do some calculations, tests. Under normal circumstances, I would say it would take a year to design and implement."

Jones stood proudly and, with his commanding voice, said, "We can't wait that long. I want every scientist and engineer at our disposal working on this. Everyone here who can help with the design, everyone on Earth and on Zalma. I want you to contact them directly, so there are no delays. I want a feasibility study in twenty-four hours. Use the best encryption available. Heck, use every encryption available, and add an extra layer that will only be used for this project, and then destroy the codes. Understood?"

Everyone in the room replied in unison, "Yes, sir!"

"Great, Mr. Howard, contact Dr. Goss. Joanua, contact the Zalma scientists. Captain Agugua, contact the Zalma Council and inform them of the change in the command structure. Ambassador Wilcox, inform the president. I will contact General Newman. If you are not involved, try to support those who are.

Make sure that they eat, and no unnecessary distractions. Dismissed."

Did I just order the creation of a black hole? A force more powerful than the sun? Never in my wildest dreams....

It was only days later that things took a turn for the worse.

"General Newman, there has been a new development. There is a seventy-three percent chance that the Moad will break through the Zalma shield in the next few days."

"How far are you away?"

"Two months."

"Oh...." Newman arched his eyebrows, thought for a moment, then straightened his uniform. *"Well, I am sure you will be glad to hear that our team is finally working well together with Dr. Goss as the new leader."*

"Glad to hear it. What else have they been working on?"

"An Electromagnetic Pulse, or EMP, shorts out any electrical systems in range, without damaging anything else. It might disable the Moad ships, and it has no effect on Zalma technology."

"Good to know. Hmm, I wonder...." Jones paced around his room. "A weapon that disables ships and doesn't hurt the occupants. I wonder if the Zalmen would consider using it?"

"It's worth a shot."

"I'll take it to Captain Agugua. *Jones out.*"

Captain Agugua was still talking to the Zalma council when Jones returned to him.

"I'll call you back," Agugua said.

"What did they say?" Jones asked.

"As I suspected, they are not fond of having weapons on our planet. They are concerned that they might hurt the Moad."

"Did you tell them that they will either kill you or take you as slaves?"

"They have forbidden me from mentioning it."

"What about if you were to disable the Moad ships, not hurt them?" Jones asked.

"What do you mean?"

"Have you heard of an Electromagnetic Pulse? It can disable their ship without hurting anyone."

"If we were to disable them, what then?" Agugua asked.

"What do you mean?"

"If we disable them, will they just die in space?"

"Yes."

"We cannot directly or indirectly cause harm to another living creature."

"But they will *kill you!*"

"We will have to take our chances."

* * *

Jones entered the conference room. "Report!"

Joanua turned multiple colors. "We have built a gravity generator and put it on a probe we launched over an hour ago. We also launched several other probes to monitor the first."

"So, what's this going to tell us?"

Mr. Howard cleared his throat. "This'll tell us if we can create the gravity of a black hole and contain it. This'll not tell us if we can build the bridge."

"Hmm. What are the expected results?"

"Either the test will succeed, or it will not create sufficient gravity," Howard said, "or the gravity will implode the probe and possibly suck us in with it."

"And the chances of that are?" Jones asked.

"Slim, but there is still a chance."

"Do we have any other options?"

The room was quiet.

"Very well," Jones said. "Proceed with the test."

Joanua turned to her screens. "Powering up the gravity generator…."

A minute passed. Lt. Cameron stayed at Joanua's side; his presence seemed to calm her as she continued the test.

"We are registering the equivalent gravity of Earth inside the probe. The gravity shielding is working, and there is no change in gravity readings outside the probe. Increasing power."

No one even dared speak as they all watched the screens.

"We are registering the gravity of the sun inside the probe. Still no change outside the probe."

Everyone in the room breathed a sigh of relief.

"Increasing power." Again, the room was silent. "We are approaching the gravity of a black hole. There are some unusual readings inside the probe."

"What kind of readings?" Jones asked.

"I don't know. The sensors are being overloaded."

"Is it the gravity?"

"I don't see how."

"The gravity outside the probe is increasing at an exponential rate. The containment is failing!"

"Shut it down!" Jones commanded.

"Too late! The probe imploded. The other probes are being sucked in! Brace for the shockwave!"

The wave hit, and people were thrown out of their seats. Cups and papers flew everywhere. The ship shook violently for about a minute.

As Jones was one of the heavier men and wasn't as affected, he looked around to see if anyone needed help. Wilcox and Edugra crawled toward each other. Joanua, who had excellent balance, gripped Cameron to steady him. Donna was thrown past him in the shockwave. When she hit the floor, she grabbed the closest solid thing nearby—Abbott—who wrapped his muscled arms around her.

Jones looked around as the ship's stabilizers came back online and the trembling stopped. "Is everyone alright?"

"We're good!" Wilcox called out. He held Edugra, running his hands soothingly up and down her arms as her colors fluctuated.

Several other confirmations came from around the room. The worst injury was a bruised elbow, about which Howard complained loudly, drawing a peel of laughter from the crew.

"What happened?" Jones asked.

Joanua went to her station. "We were pulled half a billion miles toward the temporary black hole!"

Jones looked at Howard to translate.

The scientist looked forlorn. "We failed!"

CHAPTER TWENTY-FIVE

NO WAY FORWARD

Shortly after the crew dispersed, Jones opened a video call to Gen. Newman to inform him of the results. "We're not sure when another test can be done, or if it would be worth repeating," he finished.

Newman's expression was solemn. "Yes. We were watching a relay of the test from here. No one was injured in the aftermath, I trust?"

"No."

"Good. What's the next step, then, sir?"

"I've yet to decide. We just received more bad news. The deflectors on Zalma are expected to fail in the next hour or two."

Newman's face fell. "Oh, so we really have failed."

"I am afraid so," Jones replied. "The Zalma council is still hopeful that the Moadites won't hurt them."

Newman grunted. "There is not much of a chance of that, is there?"

Jones shook his head. "Why don't you give your people the night off? They earned it. I'll do the same here."

Newman just nodded.

"And…why don't you head to your permanent base?"

"We have a permanent base?! Sir?!"

"Yes. It's probably not finished yet, but my sources tell me that Scornson's men haven't requested long range training flights in a while. Hopefully, they have given up on finding you. I'll enable you to access the rest of the route. *Jones out.*"

The call ended, and Jones turned away. He hung his head, a sigh of defeat ghosting from his lips. In front of his soldiers he had to keep up a strong front; only when he was alone could he let his burdens show.

What are we going to do now?

Jones opened his door.

Lt. Cameron entered. "Sir, during your departure speech you said you were available if we needed to talk?"

Jones nodded. "What can I do for you, Lieutenant?"

"During the shockwave, something strange happened."

"With Joanua?"

"Yes, how did you know?"

Jones closed the door. "We have been in space for several months. It's natural to want someone to talk to, or is it more than that?"

Cameron's eyes widened. "No! I mean, it just happened. I thought we were going to die, and somehow we ended up together. I don't even remember how. Is that love?"

Jones chuckled. "Maybe, maybe not. I think it's too early to tell, but that doesn't mean you can't be friends until you figure it out." Jones sighed; his heart sank. "Just be careful to keep it as friends until you both know. It's hard when one's in love, and the other isn't."

He paused. "I've seen many good people destroyed when their affections aren't returned and they settle for sex, it's an addiction. Like alcohol, they seemed happy for a short time, but then they seemed even lonelier, emptier, even obsessed with trying to make it work, but you can't make someone love you."

Cameron's eyes widened, then he stood up and shook Jones's hand. "Thank you, sir."

"Everyone to the conference room!" It was Edugra again, but this time her voice sounded happy.

When Jones arrived, Captain Agugua was standing beside the screen at the front of the room—the one that showed them live footage of the ongoing battle on Zalma. This time, though, no explosions rocked the world. The Moad ship seemed to have taken a run at the planet's deflectors, but it had bounced off. It was slowly spiraling away into space.

Agugua's smile was blinding. "The Moadites' attack stopped as our deflectors failed," he announced. "We think that they ran out of ammunition, because they flew their ship directly into the deflectors. As you can see here, that break provided enough time for the deflectors to regenerate and stop them."

Everyone breathed a sigh of relief.

"Does this mean we have another month before they return?" Lt. Cameron asked.

Agugua nodded. "We believe so."

"Great, so now all we have to do is to make this ship fly twice as fast, and then come up with a plan," Mr. Howard said.

"There is an incoming message from Zalma," Edugra announced as she read from her arm, "One of the scientists has compared the readings from the probe to the nearest black hole, and found that they matched."

"Are you saying what I think you are saying?" Wilcox asked.

"Yes," Joanua cut in, also reading her arm. "Before the probe broke up, it established a bridge to the black hole."

"So, our test was a success after all?" Jones asked.

"I still have to review the data, and there is lots of work to be done, but…." Joanua looked at Cameron, who nodded and placed a hand on her shoulder. She looked back at Jones. "Yes, we believe it will work."

"Do you understand any of this scientific terminology?" Jones asked Gen. Newman on his communicator.

Newman sat back and steepled his fingers. *"I understand the basics, but not much more."*

"Our ship has been sending out probes for a week, and we try to make contact with the probe from Earth or Zalma, and then it implodes." Jones threw up his hands.

"Yes, but it rarely links to a black hole anymore, and before it implodes, it usually links to one of the planet's probes. Also, it takes much longer for it to implode, meaning they are getting close to stabilizing it." Newman smiled.

"I hope you're right," Jones said. "At least they've installed safeties, so the implosion isn't pulling us off course anymore."

"Yes, as I understand it, they feel safe enough to bring the probe into our solar system, and hope that they can bring it into Earth's orbit soon," Newman said.

"After the experience we had with the implosion, I wouldn't be in too much of a rush. I like Earth and don't want to lose it. The Zalmen said that there's no sign of intelligent life or technology in our system, other than Earth, so I think we can continue to transmit encrypted messages at short range," Jones said.

Newman's face went pale. *"Short range? You mean to Pluto?"*

Jones chuckled. "Wow! Everything is relative, isn't it? It didn't even cross my mind that I used to consider that an unachievable distance."

* * *

After a week's worth of hard work and long hours, the day finally came.

"We did it!" Lt. Cameron proudly announced. "We formed a bridge to both Earth and Zalma!"

Jones smiled. "Good news indeed!"

"We have started to receive the Earth's team's theories and schematics." Joanua turned red. "When I saw that data on magnetizing the hull, I remembered we were going to try to make our ship faster."

"Yes, we were distracted by the black hole." Jones paused, then smirked. "It sucked all our thoughts and energy, didn't it?"

Joanua stared at him silently, turned a dark green as she digested his play on words. He saw the exact moment understanding dawned on her, as she turned red, and laughed.

Jones raised an eyebrow. "Do you think it will work? Will we be able to get there before the next attack?"

"I don't know, sir. I will have to run some tests."

The very next day, Joanua brought him even more good news. "It worked. We are traveling three times faster. We should make it in time," she said.

"Well done," Jones replied.

Captain Agugua approached Jones. "General, with

all the new weapons you are creating, the Zalma council is worried about the safety of the Moad."

Jones choked. "Did you say the safety of the Moad? Our enemy? You are worried about their safety?"

"Yes. As you know, our technology has safeties to prevent you from deliberately killing them, but what if you damage their ship beyond repair? Or one of these cannonballs you are making accidentally hits and kills someone on the ship?"

Oh boy. How do I handle this? "Captain, you know that I share your desire not to deliberately hurt anyone, but this is war. We can only do so much to stop them from attacking you without hurting them. Accidents happen, even outside of war."

Agugua changed colors many times. "Yes, but can we do anything to help them if such injuries do occur?"

"What are you proposing?"

"The council would like to send our medical people to treat their injuries, and our engineers to repair their ship," Agugua said.

Jones's heart felt like it stopped for a second or two. "If you did, the Moad would either take them hostage or kill them. I'm sorry, I can't allow that." *I have to give them some assurance, but what?* "However, I'mmmm… sure our engineers will be able to come up with a safe way to deliver medical supplies and equipment, as well as remotely repair their ship."

* * *

Jones reached out to shake Gen. Newman's hand, and stumbled forward when his hand went right through. "Wow, these three-dimensional glasses work pretty well," he said, then chuckled. "And they're not those red and blue lenses like our movies use."

Newman moved to sit down, but the chair wasn't there and he fell. Jones instinctively reached out to catch him, but his hands grasped at nothing.

Both men coughed, embarrassed.

"This is too realistic," Jones said. "We need a way to know what's really here, and what's not."

"I'm adjusting the transparency to fifty percent," Joanua said. In front of Jones, Newman's form faded, and Jones was able to see the wall through his head and torso.

The transparent Newman's eyes widened. *"General Jones, you look like a ghost."* He laughed. *"That's much better. At least we can tell the difference now."*

"Amazing, isn't it?" Jones took off the glasses, and Newman disappeared. He put them back on, and Newman's ghost was back in front of him. "Anyway, let's get down to business. The magnetized hull is working, and we expect to make it on time before the next ship arrives."

"The scientists are working well together, between your ship, Zalma, and Earth. They have refined the gravity

gun, and it has the capability to push, pull, or hold an object in place," Newman replied.

"Yes, and I hear it also has the ability to crush an object, although they tell me that the Zalmen have installed safeties so that it will not crush a living creature, or an object with one inside of it," Jones said.

"Wow! They're serious about not hurting the people who are attacking them," Newman said.

"Yes. We've had to make plans for sending the Moadites medical supplies and to remotely repair enemy ships," Jones said.

"Unbelievable. The Zalmen never cease to amaze me," Newman said.

The ship's crew and Jones's team were in the conference room with no table. Gen. Newman, Sgt. Dow, Dr. Goss, Mr. Quinn and others appeared as holograms. Everyone was wearing glasses. In the middle a hologram of the Z3 space fighter floated.

"The Z3 started with Mr. Harper's X20 design, but has gone through several revisions," Dr. Goss said. *"It's equipped with conventional Earth weaponry, such as machine guns and cannon balls…."*

"But the gunpowder doesn't ignite without oxygen," Mr. Howard added.

"Yes. We tried compressed air in with the gunpowder, but then discovered that compressed air was sufficient to push the projectile," Quinn said.

"To let the Moad know that we mean them no harm, we have installed supplies that the Moad might need for their return home into the cannon balls. The nuclear torpedo is basically a small nuclear engine that explodes on impact or is manually detonated," Dr. Goss added. "Likewise, the plasma torpedo has a nuclear engine and a plasma torch attached to the front. It should burn a hole through anything."

Jones raised his hand.

Quinn anticipated and answered his question. "But it's only enabled when permission is granted, like the EMP."

Jones nodded.

"It was easy to create the Electromagnetic Pulse. The hard part was to focus it to only disable one target at a time. But we learned from focusing the black hole to communicate." Quinn took a breath and continued. "As General Jones reminded me, we don't want the enemy to know about these technologies unless they already have them and use them against us, or as a last resort."

He scanned the room to see if anyone had questions before continuing. "The deflectors and lasers are installed and become active when the ship is damaged, conventional weapons run out of ammunition, or the ship has a human occupant and is about to receive fatal damage."

"Very good. Where are we with the repair robots?" Jones asked.

"We have built repair robots to fix any ship too damaged to fly home," Howard answered. "These repair robots will also install a sample of the technology we wish to trade. The deflectors and anti-gravity will only kick in when they set their engines to ninety percent or more, and will allow them to fly about twice as fast. The deflectors, of course, will also activate if an object is about to collide. We hope it will give them the incentive to trade."

"It will be interesting to see how they react," Ambassador Wilcox said.

"Yes it will," Jones said. "Remember everyone, we don't want them to know about our advanced technology or they will want to negotiate or steal it."

"We have only two pilots. Sergeant Abbott and I will each fly a fighter; the rest will be remotely controlled from Earth. Just like our 3D glasses, it will look like there is a pilot in them," Lt. McKenzie said.

"Also, we want the Moad to know that we are helping the pacifist Zalmen, but not who we are or where we are from. We don't want them coming to Earth any time soon. These pointy Z3's are a far cry from the Zalma box shaped ships," Jones said. "So, Captain Agugua lined us up so we appear to be coming from an empty solar system for our approach, and turned our invisibility off."

"*A good precaution, sir,*" Newman said.

"It will be interesting to see if they take the bait," Wilcox said.

With that said, the meeting was dismissed, and everyone took off their glasses.

"We are a few days from Zalma, and are matching the first Moad ship's distance from the planet. We were surprised to discover four other Moad ships rapidly decelerating in hopes of joining the first invasion. The furthest ship appears to be enduring five times their normal gravity to make it on time," Jones said.

"Wow! Do you think they will survive?" Gen. Newman asked.

"They tell me that as long as they are in a bed or chair, our computer simulations show that they should be unharmed, depending on their physiology, of course. If they're reptilian, they should be able to handle more than we do," Jones said.

Newman raised his eyebrows, impressed.

"Our people have done their jobs. Our ships and warriors are ready for battle, so I'm ordering everyone to take some well-deserved rest. I suggest having a party sooner, so your people can recover before the battle," Jones said.

Newman chuckled. *"Yes, sir."* He signed off.

Jones opened his door.

Heavy footsteps came up the hallway. They faded again, then came back. Jones looked up. It was Sgt.

Abbott, and from the sounds of it, he was agitated. "Sergeant!" Jones called.

Abbott entered quickly and saluted sharply. "Sir!"

Jones closed the door and returned the salute. Abbott lowered his hand, but he didn't look any less tense.

"What can I do for you, Sergeant?"

"You're the one who called me in, sir. What can I do for you?"

Jones kept his military stance. "You've been pacing the hallways for days. I know you're too independent to go to anyone for advice, but I really think you need some peace of mind. We have been in space for a long time, and I'm sure you're starting to feel lonely." Jones gave the sergeant a knowing look.

Abbott's eyes popped, and then he nodded.

"The black hole test was unlike anything anyone has ever experienced before. Some of us felt things we never experienced before."

Abbott grunted but reluctantly agreed.

"Now, I'm sure you know that there's no regulations against you dating a civilian. So, you must be concerned that being such a strong man, that you might hurt such a frail lady as Miss Warren."

Abbott looked at Jones with empty, almost watery eyes.

"The fact that you are concerned means you are not going to hurt her when you are in your right mind, so limit your alcohol. No matter how bad your day gets, or how much you want to celebrate, if you hit her when you're drunk, you will cause permanent injury or death and the party's over. Do you understand?"

"Yes, sir."

"And I'll put this in terms you'll understand. While love will make you strong, sex will tear you down mentally and physically. I've seen many good men doubt themselves and their worth. The next thing I know, they're taking suicide missions and not coming back."

Abbott dropped his head. "Yes, sir."

"The ones who found love would occasionally take difficult missions, but despite all odds, they came back. Make sure you know which one you're getting into. You're a good soldier, and I would hate to lose you."

Abbott's lips straightened.

That's probably as close to a smile as I'm going to get.

"Until then, there is no problem with getting to know her better. Is there anything else?"

"No, sir. Thank you, sir."

"Dismissed."

CHAPTER TWENTY-SIX

THE YMIT

THE YMIT, SPACE

Approaching Zalma.

Jones stood at the front of the Ymit's bridge.

"Ship-wide and Einstein–Rosen Bridge communications, please. I would like to talk to everyone."

Edugra tapped her touchscreen, sounding a whistle throughout the ship. The Earthlings were used to hearing this sound on battleships and requested it be added.

"This is General Jones. We are about to make interstellar history. Two planets uniting against an aggressor. As far as we know, we have the upper hand with better technology, but we don't want the Moad to know how much better our technology is, or they will be scared and try to negotiate or steal it. They know that the Zalmen have deflectors, and that's all. They don't know about us humans, and this will be our introduction. When we engage them, remember to reserve our advanced technology unless necessary. Our goals are to:

"One, stop this attack.

"Two, give them honor and pride.

"Three, establish our superior technology. Remember, as much as we would like to end this war, it's unlikely to happen today. So, let's show them, *The Galaxy's Peacekeepers*! Is everyone ready?"

Jones heard several people say, *"Yes sir"* and *"Ready"* over the radio.

"Good luck, everyone." Jones nodded at the screen. "Earth Squad, you are clear to launch!"

"Roger that."

The nineteen remote-controlled $Z3$'s detached. They had been built by the nanites, essentially grown on the outside of the Ymit. Lieutenant McKenzie and Sergeant Abbott's ships launched from the ship's hangar. They took flanking positions.

"Zalma colony ship. Are you ready?"

The ship was unarmed; it was built to move Zalma's population to New Zalma but it hadn't had a chance to leave. That's not why it was there. Its size was the perfect intimidation tool. With its deflectors, it would seem virtually indestructible.

"Ready," came the reply.

"Remember, no invisibility. We don't want them to know we have that. And you don't have to do anything but look big."

"*Understood, General. After all these years, it will be a pleasure to see the attacks come to an end.*"

"It's a pleasure to be here. We'll call you if we need you." Jones gave Edugra the signal to close the channel.

The first Moad ship slowed as they saw the Ymit. The other four ships were approaching fast at different speeds and reversed, with the main engines on full to stop.

As they neared the first ship, the engines ceased, and the vessels turned forward, ready for battle.

"Open the Moad frequency and turn on the translator."

Edugra nodded.

"Moad ships. You have entered Zalma's space and are ordered to turn around." Jones listened for a minute, but there was no reply. He repeated the message with the same result. "Moad ships. You have entered Zalma's space. If you attack, we will return fire. Do you understand?"

"*Plan Eight,*" was the response from one of the Moad captains.

"That was encrypted," Edugra confirmed.

"Yes, they don't know we can decrypt their messages, but we don't know what 'Plan Eight' is either."

The five Moad ships changed course and headed for the Ymit, and they were not stopping.

Jones's previous simulations had indicated that if a Moad ship rammed the Ymit at low speed, the ship would bounce off the deflector. At high speed, the Moad ship would be destroyed, but the Ymit would not be damaged. But he never anticipated five Moad ships. He wondered if they would survive.

"Fighters pull back. It looks like we are in for a game of chicken. Do not fire until fired upon." Jones turned around. "Captain Agugua, what is our distance?"

"500 miles and closing," the captain announced. "400 miles.... 300.... 200.... 100.... They are veering off."

Several flashes illuminated the screen as the Moad bombs detonated.

"Status report!" Jones barked out.

"All five ships released bombs as they veered. They detonated against our deflectors with no damage. The bombs do not appear to have propulsion. The fighters were not targeted and are not damaged," Mr. Howard reported.

"Lieutenant McKenzie, break off and engage," Jones ordered.

"*Machine guns. Fire,*" was the response over the radio.

Jones was thankful McKenzie and Abbott were the only two pilots in space. The Earth pilots had about a tenth-of-a-second delay in their movements. Since Abbott was new to flying, he could use voice commands for things like takeoff and landing.

"Captain, bring us about."

A single fighter detached from each of the Moad main ships. McKenzie's squadron engaged them.

The Moad fighters, as well as their main ship gun turrets, fired.

"I'm hit. Minor damage. Disabling affected systems," one of the remote pilots said.

When McKenzie's group finished their pass, Jones noticed the primary ships were damaged and losing air. Then he noticed that the enemy fighters were not following their fighters. One of the main Moad ships fired at them.

"Torpedo! Evasive maneuvers!" McKenzie called.

There was a flash of bright light between the fighters as a nuclear explosive detonated.

Two of the fighters were destroyed, and the others were spinning out of control in different directions.

"Lieutenant McKenzie, damage report!" Jones called out, but there was silence. "Sergeant Abbott, damage report!" The silence continued. "Come in, Lieutenant McKenzie! Sergeant Abbott?"

The tense silence continued for about a minute before McKenzie's voice replied. *"I'm OK. The blast damaged our traditional systems and weapons. Switching to Zalma backups."*

"I'm OK too," Abbott said.

The fighters stopped spinning and once again focused on the enemy ships.

"Torpedo launched! Deflectors to maximum! Evasive maneuvers!"

Once again, there was another flash of light as a torpedo detonated, but this time the fighters had no problem evading it.

"The deflectors worked. No damage. I'm out of bullets. Switching to lasers."

McKenzie flew through enemy fighters as he dodged bullets and lasers. One of the Z3's exploded.

He got close to one of the Moad main ships, launching cannonballs, causing air to vent as they passed through and some small fires that extinguished quickly.

McKenzie damaged a Moad fighter, main ship gun turret, and torpedo tube. The damaged enemy fighter limped back to its main ship.

They lost another three Z3's.

From the bridge, Jones saw the occasional arcs of light as weapons and projectiles bounced off the Z3's deflectors.

They made several more passes and lost another eight Z3's, but the Moad main ship weapons were disabled.

One Moad fighter remained and was chasing Abbott. *"McKenzie, where are you?"*

"I'm on my way."

The three ships zigzagged across space.

"He's too close. I can't get a shot without hitting you," McKenzie said.

Abbott turned his fighter and headed directly for one of the Moad main ships.

"Abbott! Pull up!" Ambassador Wilcox shouted.

"Not yet," Abbott replied.

Donna was holding Wilcox's arm tight. Abbott's ship was on a collision course with the Moad main ship.

"Pull up!" Wilcox shouted.

"Not yet," Abbott replied.

Just before Abbott's fighter hit, he did an incredibly sharp turn.

"Wahoo! This thing can really fly!" Abbott announced through the radio.

Donna let out a sigh of relief. "Where did he learn that?"

Howard chuckled. "That was one of the maneuvers we programmed into his flight computer."

"Sorry to scare you," Cameron added.

Donna's face was white, and she quickly strode off the bridge.

The Moad fighter couldn't match the angle of the Z3, and scratched the surface before continuing pursuit.

"McKenzie, what's taking you so long? Get this guy off my butt," Abbott grumbled.

McKenzie was shooting, but couldn't get a hit. *"This pilot is good. Are you sure we can't just destroy this guy?"* he asked.

"Negative," Jones replied.

"Permission to use EMP?"

"Permission granted."

The Moad fighter suddenly lost power and was floating. McKenzie had to react fast to avoid a collision.

McKenzie's voice came over the radio. *"Mission accomplished. All enemy ship weapons disabled."*

The Moad main ship's engines lit up, and they tilted toward the planet. They each dropped a massive number of bombs, aiming toward the planet.

"Zalma colony ship, it looks like they are going to try breaking through. Be prepared to intercept the enemy ships and push them back into space." Jones was right, the deflectors failed, and the Moad ships made a run at the openings.

The giant ship lifted off from the planet, intercepting, and using its deflector, it pushed the enemy ships back into orbit, before dipping below the deflectors as they regenerated. Jones could not comprehend the size of the colony vessel. It was at least one hundred times larger than the Ymit, maybe even one thousand times.

The Zalma colony ship blocked their view of the planet.

The Moad ships remained motionless, except for their artificial gravity Ferris wheels, and it looked like the venting air holes were being patched. They had no weapons, and their transparent shields were badly damaged.

"Moad frequency and translation, please." Jones looked at Edugra, who nodded. "Moad ships. You are outnumbered and outgunned. Surrender!"

Edugra closed the channel.

They could hear the Moad captains arguing with each other.

"Repair your ships. Prepare for another bombing run. Spread out."

"My ship is too damaged. We must retreat."

"Yes, retreat."

"Stay and fight, you coward!"

"Fight!"

Jones shook his head. "All fighters. Re-engage."

As soon as the fighters turned to the Moad ships, one of their engines lit up and broke orbit.

After the fighters fired a few shots, the second Moad ship also broke orbit.

"Cowards! Get back here!" a Moad captain yelled.

The three remaining Moad ships took heavy damage, and another one left, and soon another.

The last Moad ship managed to get some weapons working, and returned fire, but was soon disabled again. Its engine lit up briefly but failed several times.

"The last ship has sustained too much damage," Joanua said.

"Shall we help them out?" Jones asked.

"Activating repair robots."

The repair robots detached from the Ymit and flew toward the damaged Moad ship. Some carried the gift engines and deflectors.

Jones watched what looked like little torpedoes and chuckled. "The Moad probably think we are going to finish them off. Won't they be surprised?"

After about half an hour, the air venting from the damaged ship stopped, and Joanua reported that they were successfully pumping in new air. *That should let the Moad captain know that he's not in any danger.*

About another half an hour later, Joanua announced that the sample deflector and artificial gravity had been installed. The nuclear engine was the hardest to fix and took another hour. As soon as Joanua announced that it was fixed, the engine lit up.

The repair bots returned to the Ymit with the fighters. The two pilots landed in the hangar, while the other fighters attached to the outside.

The Moad ship broke orbit.

"Moad frequency, please," Jones ordered.

Edugra nodded.

"We wish you a safe trip home. You may have noticed that the bombshells contain food and medical supplies." Jones waited for a reply, but the Moad were silent.

"What, nothing to say?" Jones signaled to Edugra again.

"Channel closed."

A voice came through the Moad channel and was translated. *"Hey, what about me?"*

"Who said that?" Jones asked.

"The damaged fighter. They are leaving without him," Edugra said.

"Captain Agugua, can you pick it up?" Jones asked.

"Yes."

"Sergeant Abbott." Jones paused while Edugra connected to him. After Jones heard his voice repeated, he said, "Prepare to receive a guest in the hangar."

"It's about time."

Agugua maneuvered the Ymit in front of the Moad fighter and matched its speed. As the Ymit slowed down, they could see on the screen the Moad fighter enter the hangar and landed with a thud. Agugua closed the outside doors and pressurized the room. Abbott entered and swung a baseball bat over his shoulder.

The Moad fighter's cabin opened, and a Jurassic bird-like being exited the ship.

The two warriors stared at each other for a minute, then circled. Abbott stopped, then ran toward the bird with the bat. The bird extended a spiked wing and easily threw Abbott against the wall. When he shook himself off, he noticed blood dripping from his forehead and grinned.

"He likes a challenge," Jones explained to Agugua.

Abbott ran again but ducked before the wing hit him. He swung the bat at the bird's chest, and the bird brought in its wings.

Jones couldn't see Abbott, but judging by the way the bird was twitching, Abbott was putting up a good fight. Then the wings opened wide, and Jones saw the blue light of Abbott's plasma dagger.

The bird waved a wing toward Abbott's legs but quickly retreated when he moved the dagger to intercept.

Abbott held the dagger up, and the bird backed toward the wall and sat down.

On the bridge, Wilcox was watching on the screen, and he nodded to Edugra to open a channel. "Your people have left you. You have no place to go," he said.

The bird looked around, wondering where the voice was coming from. A video feed from the bridge appeared on the wall.

Jones wondered if the translators worked. After about a minute the bird replied in squawks. It was a different sound than the reptilian language the Moad used. The squawks repeated and repeated, then the bird made the reptilian clicks which the computer translated. *"They are not my people. I don't have people."*

"I see that. You don't look like the reptiles we saw in the video from the original probe."

Again the bird squawked, then clicked. *"No, I have not seen anyone like myself since I was young."*

"Not since you were young?"

The bird squawked, and the computer immediately translated. *"No."*

"That must be sad."

The bird squawked, then clicked. *"Yes, sad."*

"Were you a prisoner?"

"They treated me well, as long as I did what they said. When I didn't, they hurt me."

"Well, as long as you don't hurt us, we won't hurt you. OK?"

Abbott looked up at the video feed and grunted.

"OK," the bird replied.

Abbott begrudgingly put his plasma dagger away and left the hangar.

Jones looked at Edugra.

"Our audio is turned off," she told him.

"Is he secure in there?" Jones asked.

"Yes, he has no place to go, and he can't damage anything," Agugua replied.

The Jurassic would squawk, then click in the reptilian language, then the computer would translate a word.

Wilcox's eyes popped. "It's training our translator with its language."

Jones turned to Wilcox. "Impressive." Then he turned to Agugua. "It can't access any of our personal or military information, can it?"

Agugua turned to Joanua. "Please make sure its access is restricted."

CHARLIE BAKER: EPISODE 1

"Thank you," Jones said. He addressed the people on the bridge. "Our mission is complete!"

A cheer broke out.

"Captain, please take us home," Jones said.

"To Earth?" Agugua asked, looking at him with a crinkled forehead.

"No, sorry. Your home."

Agugua nodded. "Yes, sir!"

CHAPTER TWENTY-SEVEN

ZALMA

THE PLANET ZALMA

As the Ymit touched down, millions of cheering Zalmen crowded around the landing pad. The door opened, and the Zalmen crew went out first to greet the council. Then they all turned to the ship.

"Introducing our Earth heroes. First: General Frank Jones."

The crowd cheered as the general exited and greeted the council with a bow. They introduced the others in order of rank.

Jones addressed the crowd. "Thank you. We are glad to be of service. However, I fear that the war is not yet over. The Moad ships were designed for bombardment, not for defense. We caught them off guard. We may have won this battle, however, they are likely to return and in greater numbers, but we will be ready!"

DID YOU ENJOY THIS BOOK?

Your feedback helps me provide the best quality books and helps other readers like you discover them.

It would mean the world to me if you took two minutes to share your thoughts about this book. You can leave a review with the retailer of your choice and/or send an email to *tony@tonybrichard.com* with your honest feedback.

Thank you, I really appreciate it.

ACKNOWLEDGMENTS

Thank you to everyone who has helped this book become a reality. To my wife, Lydia, without whom this wouldn't be possible, to my Beta readers, to Lesia for designing the cover, to Carolin Petersen for editing and adding all of the final touches, and to every person who pitched in their ideas and opinions.

A special thanks to Gene Roddenberry, George Lucas, Dean Devlin, Roland Emmerich, Brad Wright, Jonathan Glassner, Ronald D. Moore, Ben Nedivi, Matt Wolpert, Greg Berlanti, and Todd Helbing for their wonderful creations (Star Trek, Star Wars, Stargate, For All Mankind, and Superman and Lois) that have and continue to inspire me.

PRONUNCIATION GUIDE

Ymit	YEM—it
Geogram	Ge—OG—ram
Agugua	A—GU—gwa
Joanua	Jo—ANN—wa
Edugra	Ed—OOO—gra
Sarara	Sa—RARE—ah
Kanara	Can—AR—ah
Zalma	ZALL—mah
Zalmen	ZALL—men
Moad	Moe—ADD
Moadites	Moe—ADD—eytes

SERIES TIMELINE

ROSWELL: FIRST CONTACT
Malcolm Dow & Adam Rabinowitz: Episode 1

NEGOTIATIONS
Ryan Wilcox: Episode 1

THE GOOD, THE BAD, AND THE UNDECIDED
Greg Newman: Episode 1

DEFYING GRAVITY
Mary Goss: Episode 1

(spanning the entire timeline)

CHARLIE'S BIG CHANCE   THE WOUNDLESS WAR
Charlie Baker: Episode 1   *Frank Jones: Episode 1*

FROM ROSWELL TO AREA 51: THE NOVEL
(a single "cinematic cut" that braids all six POVs in chronological order)

Earth's Secret Alliance is a series of clean,
family friendly, uplifting,
one-to-two-hour short stories.

ROSWELL: FIRST CONTACT

When Private Malcolm Dow went to clean up a crashed weather balloon, hey came face-to-face with an alien instead.

Adam Rabinowitz was one of those wimps who followed Dow around, hoping for protection from the bullies.

While Dow was reluctant, Rabinowitz instantly took on the Alien's plight – military help for his besieged planet, Zalma. But when he gets caught, it's up to Dow to save the day.

If they fail, it's not just Zalma; Earth may be captured or destroyed next. But if they are to succeed, they must work around the chain of command to avoid the anti-alien majority.

NEGOTIATIONS

The Zalmen have arrived on Earth hungry for collaboration. But they're about to lose their appetite.

In 1947, a peaceful day at home for talented negotiator Ryan Wilcox is rudely interrupted by a phone call from the president. With the help of General Jones and Malcolm Dow, he's to arrange an interplanetary alliance. It's an opportunity that Earth can't afford to miss. The aliens offer knowledge that will speed up the Human advance by hundreds of years.

But as with any friendship, the beginning stages require a delicate approach. And there's one issue of "delicacy" that threatens to turn their partnership into an outright war.

Will Ryan the wordsmith rise to the challenge and find common ground? Or is it the end of life as we know it?

THE GOOD, THE BAD, AND THE UNDECIDED

Major General Greg Newman has always been self-centered and opportunistic-even using WWII as a stepping stone to advance his career. Now that the war is over, he's looking for a new way to add more stars to his shoulders. Soon Greg is approached about a secret mission spying on a superior officer and a classified research facility. He hopes this job will land him that quick promotion but has reservations about surveilling this officer. Voicing his concern is only met with not-so-subtle threats.

Now entangled in a diabolical plan, Greg questions which boundaries he's unwilling to cross. If he doesn't jettison his morals entirely, then his career will surely go down in flames. Greg must decide who to trust, and that becomes a choice between a quick promotion, or saving his country—and maybe even the world.

DEFYING GRAVITY

In 1947, there's an alien invasion looming and humankind's best hope is a brilliant nineteen-year-old woman.

When the A-bomb ended the war, with a power unlike anything humans had ever witnessed, Mary Goss was driven to gain the knowledge to prevent another war from ever beginning. Now the Army has come calling, looking for "a few good men" for a top-secret project. Instead, they find that the best and brightest is Mary.

Much to Mary's horror, the project reveals an alien invasion. Yet at every turn, her efforts to intervene are thwarted by small-minded engineers who can't look past her gender and age. She'd dealt with her fair share of discrimination in university, but with the fate of the world on the line, there isn't time to waste on petty differences.

CHARLIE'S BIG CHANCE

Aliens. A notebook. A secret no one will believe.

Charlie Baker is 12 years old, dreams of being a reporter, and uses a wheelchair to get around her small town. When she stumbles across a crashed alien ship near Roswell, everything changes.

Now Charlie has a chance to write the story of a lifetime—but telling the truth might put the aliens in danger. Can she keep their secret, even as the military closes in?

  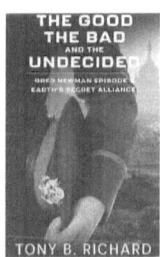

ABOUT THE AUTHOR

Tony B. Richard lives in Langley, British Columbia. He is a computer programmer (coder) and instructor. This grand adventure has been in his head for decades, and during the Covid-19 pandemic, he thought it was finally time to put it down on paper.

"Differences are something to be celebrated, not feared."

—TONY B. RICHARD

YOU CAN CONTACT HIM WITH QUESTIONS OR COMMENTS AT:

Website: www.tonybrichard.com
Email: tony@tonybrichard.com
Facebook: EarthsSecretAlliance
Twitter: @TonyBRichard1
Instagram: tony_b_richard
Goodreads: Tony B. Richard

www.ingramcontent.com/pod-product-compliance
Lightning Source LLC
Chambersburg PA
CBHW032120170626
46808CB00006B/2038